THE PROFESSOR'S

HOUSE

ALSO BY WILLA CATHER

WILLA CATHER

The Professor's House

Vintage Classics

VINTAGE BOOKS
A DIVISION OF RANDOM HOUSE, INC., NEW YORK

VINTAGE CLASSICS EDITION, NOVEMBER 1990

Copyright 1925 by Willa Cather
Copyright renewed 1953 by Edith Lewis and
The City Bank Farmers Trust Co.

Library of Congress Cataloging-in-Publication Data
Cather, Willa, 1873–1947.
The professor's house / Willa Cather.
p. cm.—(Vintage classics)
ISBN 0-679-73180-6 (pbk.)
I. Title. II. Series.
PS3505.A87P7 1990
813'.52—dc20 90-50269
CIP

BOOK DESIGN BY ANN GOLD

Manufactured in the United States of America
13579C86420

"A turquoise set in silver, wasn't it? . . .
Yes, a turquoise set in dull silver."
—*Louie Marsellus*

CONTENTS

BOOK ONE

The Family

ONE

The moving was over and done. Professor St. Peter was alone in the dismantled house where he had lived ever since his marriage, where he had worked out his career and brought up his two daughters. It was almost as ugly as it is possible for a house to be; square, three stories in height, painted the colour of ashes—the front porch just too narrow for comfort, with a slanting floor and sagging steps. As he walked slowly about the empty, echoing rooms on that bright September morning, the Professor regarded thoughtfully the needless inconveniences he had put up with for so long; the stairs that were too steep, the halls that were too cramped, the awkward oak mantles with thick round posts crowned by bumptious wooden balls, over green-tiled fire-places.

Certain wobbly stair treads, certain creaky boards in the upstairs hall, had made him wince many times a day for twenty-odd years—and they still creaked and wobbled. He had a deft hand with tools, he could easily have fixed them, but there were always so many things to fix, and there was not time enough to go round. He went into the kitchen, where he had carpentered under a succession of cooks, went up to the bath-room on the second floor, where there was only a painted tin tub; the taps were so old that no plumber could ever screw them tight enough to stop the drip, the window could only be coaxed up and down by wriggling, and the doors of the linen closet didn't fit. He had sympathized with his daughters' dissatisfaction, though he could never quite agree with them that the bath should be the most attractive room in the house. He had spent the happiest years of his youth in a house at Versailles where it distinctly was not, and he had known many charming people who had no bath at all. However, as his wife said: "If your country has contributed one thing, at least, to civilization, why not have it?" Many a night, after blowing out his study lamp, he had leaped into that tub, clad in his pyjamas, to give it another coat of some one of the many paints that were advertised to behave like porcelain, and didn't.

The Professor in pyjamas was not an unpleasant sight; for looks, the fewer clothes he had on, the better. Anything that clung to his body showed it to be built upon extremely good bones, with the slender hips and springy shoulders of a tireless swimmer. Though he was born on Lake Michigan, of mixed stock (Canadian French on one side, and American farmers on the other), St. Peter was commonly said to look like a Spaniard. That was possibly because he had been in Spain a good deal, and was an authority on certain phases of Spanish history. He had a long brown face, with an oval chin over which he wore a close-trimmed Van Dyke, like a tuft of shiny black fur. With this silky, very black hair, he had a tawny skin with gold lights in it, a hawk nose, and hawk-like eyes—brown and gold and green. They were set in ample cavities, with plenty of room to move about, under thick, curly, black eyebrows that turned up sharply at the outer ends, like military moustaches. His wicked-looking eyebrows made his students call him Mephistopheles—and there was no evading the searching eyes underneath them; eyes that in a flash could pick out a friend or an unusual stranger from a throng. They had lost none of their fire, though just now the man behind them was feeling a diminution of ardour.

His daughter Kathleen, who had done several successful studies of him in water-colour, had once said:— "The thing that really makes Papa handsome is the modelling of his head between the top of his ear and his crown; it is quite the best thing about him." That part of his head was high, polished, hard as bronze, and the close-growing black hair threw off a streak of light along the rounded ridge where the skull was fullest. The mould of his head on the side was so individual and definite, so far from casual, that it was more like a statue's head than a man's.

From one of the dismantled windows the Professor happened to look out into his back garden, and at that cheerful sight he went quickly downstairs and escaped from the dusty air and brutal light of the empty rooms.

His walled-in garden had been the comfort of his life—and it was the one thing his neighbours held against him. He started to make it soon after the birth of his first daughter, when his wife began to be unreasonable about his spending so much time at the lake and on the tennis court. In this undertaking he got help and encouragement from his landlord, a retired German farmer, good-natured and lenient about everything but spending money. If the Professor happened to have a new baby at home, or a faculty dinner, or an illness in the family, or any unusual expense, Appelhoff cheerfully waited for the rent; but pay for repairs he would not. When it was a question of the garden, however, the old man sometimes stretched a point. He helped his tenant with seeds and slips and sound advice, and with his twisted old back. He even spent a little money to bear half the expense of the stucco wall.

The Professor had succeeded in making a French garden in Hamilton. There was not a blade of grass; it was a tidy half-acre of glistening gravel and glistening shrubs and bright flowers. There were trees, of course; a spreading horse-chestnut, a row of slender Lombardy poplars at the back, along the white wall, and in the middle two symmetrical, round-topped linden-trees. Masses of green-brier grew in the corners, the prickly stems interwoven and clipped until they were like great bushes. There was a bed for salad herbs. Salmon-pink geraniums dripped over the wall. The French marigolds and dahlias were just now at their best—such dahlias as no one else in Hamilton could grow. St. Peter had tended this bit of ground for over twenty years, and had got the upper hand of it. In the spring, when homesickness for other lands and the fret of things unaccomplished awoke, he worked off his discontent here. In the long hot summers, when he could not go abroad, he stayed at home with his garden, sending his wife and daughters to Colorado to escape the humid prairie heat, so nourishing to wheat and corn, so exhausting to human beings. In those months when he was a bachelor again, he brought down his books and papers and worked in a deck chair under the linden-trees; breakfasted and lunched and had his tea in the garden. And it was there he and Tom Outland used to sit and talk half through the warm, soft nights.

On this September morning, however, St. Peter knew that he could not evade the unpleasant effects of change by tarrying among his autumn flowers. He must plunge in like a man, and get used to the feeling that under his work-room there was a dead, empty house. He broke off a geranium blossom, and with it still in his hand went resolutely up two flights of stairs to the third floor where, under the slope of the mansard roof, there was one room still furnished—that is, if it had ever been furnished.

The low ceiling sloped down on three sides, the slant being interrupted on the east by a single square window, swinging outward on hinges and held ajar by a hook in the sill. This was the sole opening for light and air. Walls and ceiling alike were covered with a yellow paper which had once been very ugly, but had faded into inoffensive neutrality. The matting on the floor was worn and scratchy. Against the wall stood an old walnut table, with one leaf up, holding piles of orderly papers. Before it was a cane-backed office chair that turned on a screw. This dark den had for many years been the Professor's study.

Downstairs, off the back parlour, he had a show study, with roomy shelves where his library was housed, and a proper desk at which he wrote letters. But it was a sham. This was the place where he worked. And not he alone. For three weeks in the fall, and again three in the spring, he shared his cuddy with Augusta, the sewing-woman, niece of his old landlord, a reliable, methodical spinster, a German Catholic and very devout.

Since Augusta finished her day's work at five o'clock, and the Professor, on week-days, worked here only at night, they did not elbow each other too much. Besides, neither was devoid of consideration. Every evening, before she left, Augusta swept up the scraps from the floor, rolled her patterns, closed the sewing-machine, and picked ravellings off the box-couch, so that there would be no threads to stick to the Professor's old smoking-jacket if he should happen to lie down for a moment in working-hours.

St. Peter, in his turn, when he put out his lamp after midnight, was careful to brush away ashes and tobacco crumbs—smoking was very distasteful to Augusta—and to open the hinged window back as far as it would go, on the second hook, so that the night wind might carry away the smell of his pipe as much as possible. The unfinished dresses which she left hanging on the forms, however, were often so saturated with smoke that he knew she found it a trial to work on them next morning.

These "forms" were the subject of much banter between them. The one which Augusta called "the bust" stood in the darkest corner of the room, upon a high wooden chest in which blankets and winter wraps were yearly stored. It was a headless, armless female torso, covered with strong black cotton, and so richly developed in the part for which it was named that the Professor once explained to Augusta how, in calling it so, she followed a natural law of language, termed, for convenience, metonymy. Augusta enjoyed the Professor when he was *risqué,* since she was sure of his ultimate delicacy. Though this figure looked so ample and billowy (as if you might lay your head upon its deep-breathing softness and rest safe forever), if you touched it you suffered a severe shock, no matter how many times you had touched it before. It presented the most unsympathetic surface imaginable. Its hardness was not that of wood, which responds to concussion with living vibration and is stimulating to the hand, nor that of felt, which drinks something from the fingers. It was a dead, opaque, lumpy solidity, like chunks of putty, or tightly packed sawdust—very disappointing to the tactile sense, yet somehow always fooling you again. For no matter how often you had bumped up against that torso, you could never believe that contact with it would be as bad as it was.

The second form was more self-revelatory; a full-length female figure in a smart wire skirt with a trim metal waist line. It had no legs, as one could see all too well, no viscera behind its glistening ribs, and its bosom resembled a strong wire bird-cage. But St. Peter contended that it had a nervous system. When Augusta left it clad for the night in a new party dress for Rosamond or Kathleen, it often took on a sprightly, tricky air, as if it were going out for the evening to make a great show of being harum-scarum, giddy, *folle*. It seemed just on the point of tripping downstairs, or on tiptoe, waiting for the waltz to begin. At times the wire lady was most convincing in her pose as a woman of light behaviour, but she never fooled St. Peter. He had his blind spots, but he had never been taken in by one of her kind!

Augusta had somehow got it into her head that these forms were unsuitable companions for one engaged in scholarly pursuits, and she periodically apologized for their presence when she came to install herself and fulfil her "time" at the house.

"Not at all, Augusta," the Professor had often said. "If they were good enough for *Monsieur Bergeret*, they are certainly good enough for me."

This morning, as St. Peter was sitting in his desk chair, looking musingly at the pile of papers before him, the door opened and there stood Augusta herself. How astonishing that he had not heard her heavy, deliberate tread on the now uncarpeted stair!

"Why, Professor St. Peter! I never thought of finding you here, or I'd have knocked. I guess we will have to do our moving together."

St. Peter had risen—Augusta loved his manners—but he offered her the sewing-machine chair and resumed his seat.

"Sit down, Augusta, and we'll talk it over. I'm not moving just yet—don't want to disturb all my papers. I'm staying on until I finish a piece of writing. I've seen your uncle about it. I'll work here, and board at the new house. But this is confidential. If it were noised about, people might begin to say that Mrs. St. Peter and I had—how do they put it, parted, separated?"

Augusta dropped her eyes in an indulgent smile. "I think people in your station would say separated."

"Exactly; a good scientific term, too. Well, we haven't, you know. But I'm going to write on here for a while."

"Very well, sir. And I won't always be getting in your way now. In the new house you have a beautiful study downstairs, and I have a light, airy room on the third floor."

"Where you won't smell smoke, eh?"

"Oh, Professor, I never really minded!" Augusta spoke with feeling. She rose and took up the black bust in her long arms.

The Professor also rose, very quickly. "What are you doing?"

She laughed. "Oh, I'm not going to carry them

through the street, Professor! The grocery boy is downstairs with his cart, to wheel them over."

"Wheel them over?"

"Why, yes, to the new house, Professor. I've come a week before my regular time, to make curtains and hem linen for Mrs. St. Peter. I'll take everything over this morning except the sewing-machine—that's too heavy for the cart, so the boy will come back for it with the delivery wagon. Would you just open the door for me, please?"

"No, I won't! Not at all. You don't need her to make curtains. I can't have this room changed if I'm going to work here. He can take the sewing-machine—yes. But put her back on the chest where she belongs, please. She does very well there." St. Peter had got to the door, and stood with his back against it.

Augusta rested her burden on the edge of the chest.

"But next week I'll be working on Mrs. St. Peter's clothes, and I'll need the forms. As the boy's here, he'll just wheel them over," she said soothingly.

"I'm damned if he will! They shan't be wheeled. They stay right there in their own place. You shan't take away my ladies. I never heard of such a thing!"

Augusta was vexed with him now, and a little ashamed of him. "But, Professor, I can't work without my forms. They've been in your way all these years, and you've always complained of them, so don't be contrary, sir."

"I never complained, Augusta. Perhaps of certain

disappointments they recalled, or of cruel biological necessities they imply—but of them individually, never! Go and buy some new ones for your airy atelier, as many as you wish—I'm said to be rich now, am I not?— Go buy, but you can't have my women. That's final."

Augusta looked down her nose as she did at church when the dark sins were mentioned. "Professor," she said severely, "I think this time you are carrying a joke too far. You never used to." From the tilt of her chin he saw that she felt the presence of some improper suggestion.

"No matter what you think, you can't have them." They considered, both were in earnest now. Augusta was first to break the defiant silence.

"I suppose I am to be allowed to take my patterns?"

"Your patterns? Oh, yes, the cut-out things you keep in the couch with my old note-books? Certainly, you can have them. Let me lift it for you." He raised the hinged top of the box-couch that stood against the wall, under the slope of the ceiling. At one end of the up-holstered box were piles of note-books and bundles of manuscript tied up in square packages with mason's cord. At the other end were many little rolls of patterns, cut out of newspapers and tied with bits of ribbon, gingham, silk, georgette; notched charts which fol-lowed the changing stature and figures of the Misses St. Peter from early childhood to womanhood. In the middle of the box, patterns and manuscripts interpen-etrated.

"I see we shall have some difficulty in separating our life work, Augusta. We've kept our papers together a long while now."

"Yes, Professor. When I first came to sew for Mrs. St. Peter, I never thought I should grow grey in her service."

He started. What other future could Augusta possibly have expected? This disclosure amazed him.

"Well, well, we mustn't think mournfully of it, Augusta. Life doesn't turn out for any of us as we plan." He stood and watched her large slow hands travel about among the little packets, as she put them into his wastebasket to carry them down to the cart. He had often wondered how she managed to sew with hands that folded and unfolded as rigidly as umbrellas—no light French touch about Augusta; when she sewed on a bow, it stayed there. She herself was tall, large-boned, flat and stiff, with a plain, solid face, and brown eyes not destitute of fun. As she knelt by the couch, sorting her patterns, he stood beside her, his hand on the lid, though it would have stayed up unsupported. Her last remark had troubled him.

"What a fine lot of hair you have, Augusta! You know I think it's rather nice, that grey wave on each side. Gives it character. You'll never need any of this false hair that's in all the shop windows."

"There's altogether too much of that, Professor. So many of my customers are using it now—ladies you wouldn't expect would. They say most of it was cut off the heads of dead Chinamen. Really, it's got to be such a frequent thing that the priest spoke against it only last Sunday."

"Did he, indeed? Why, what could he say? Seems such a personal matter."

"Well, he said it was getting to be a scandal in the Church, and a priest couldn't go to see a pious woman any more without finding switches and rats and transformations lying about her room, and it was disgusting."

"Goodness gracious, Augusta! What business has a priest going to see a woman in the room where she takes off these ornaments—or to see her without them?"

Augusta grew red, and tried to look angry, but her laugh narrowly missed being a giggle. "He goes to give them the Sacrament, of course, Professor! You've made up your mind to be contrary to-day, haven't you?"

"You relieve me greatly. Yes, I suppose in cases of sudden illness the hair would be lying about where it was lightly taken off. But as you first quoted the priest, Augusta, it was rather shocking. You'll never convert me back to the religion of my fathers now, if you're going to sew in the new house and I'm going to work on here. Who is ever to remind me when it's All Souls' day, or Ember day, or Maundy Thursday, or anything?"

Augusta said she must be leaving. St. Peter heard her well-known tread as she descended the stairs. How much she reminded him of, to be sure! She had been most at the house in the days when his daughters were little girls and needed so many clean frocks. It was in those very years that he was beginning his great work; when the desire to do it and the difficulties attending such a project strove together in his mind like Macbeth's two spent swimmers—years when he had the courage to say to himself: "I will do this dazzling, this beautiful, this utterly impossible thing!"

During the fifteen years he had been working on his *Spanish Adventurers in North America,* this room had been his centre of operations. There had been delightful excursions and digressions; the two Sabbatical years when he was in Spain studying records, two summers in the South-west on the trail of his adventurers, another in Old Mexico, dashes to France to see his fosterbrothers. But the notes and the records and the ideas always came back to this room. It was here they were digested and sorted, and woven into their proper place in his history.

Fairly considered, the sewing-room was the most inconvenient study a man could possibly have, but it was the one place in the house where he could get isolation, insulation from the engaging drama of domestic life. No one was tramping over him, and only a vague sense, generally pleasant, of what went on below came up the narrow stairway. There were certainly no other advantages. The furnace heat did not reach the third floor. There was no way to warm the sewing-room, except by a rusty, round gas stove with no flue—a stove which consumed gas imperfectly and contaminated the air. To remedy this, the window must be left open—otherwise, with the ceiling so low, the air would speedily become unfit to breathe. If the stove were turned down, and the window left open little way, a sudden gust of wind would blow the wretched thing out altogether, and a deeply absorbed man might be asphyxiated before he knew it. The Professor had found that the best method, in winter, was to turn the gas on full and keep the window wide on the hook, even if he had to put on a leather jacket over his working-coat. By that arrangement he had somehow managed to get air enough to work by.

He wondered now why he had never looked about for a better stove, a newer model; or why he had not at least painted this one, flaky with rust. But he had been able to get on only by neglecting negative comforts. He was by no means an ascetic. He knew that he was terribly selfish about personal pleasures, fought for them. If a thing gave him delight, he got it, if he sold his shirt for it. By doing without many so-called necessities he had managed to have his luxuries. He might, for instance, have had a convenient electric drop-light attached to the socket above his writing-table. Preferably he wrote by a faithful kerosene lamp which he filled and tended himself. But sometimes he found that the oil-can in the closet was empty; then, to get more, he would have had to go down through the house to the cellar, and on his way he would almost surely become interested in what the children were doing, or in what his wife was doing—or he would notice that the kitchen linoleum was breaking under the sink where the maid kicked it up, and he would stop to tack it down. On that perilous journey down through the human house he might lose his mood, his enthusiasm, even his temper. So when the lamp was empty—and that usually occurred when he was in the middle of a most important passage—he jammed an eyeshade on his forehead and worked by the glare of that tormenting pear-shaped bulb, sticking out of the wall on a short curved neck just about four feet above his table. It was hard on eyes even as good as his. But once at his desk, he didn't dare quit it. He had found that you can train the mind to be active at a fixed time, just as the stomach is trained to be hungry at certain hours of the day.

If someone in the family happened to be sick, he didn't go to his study at all. Two evenings of the week he spent with his wife and daughters, and one evening he and his wife went out to dinner, or to the theatre or a concert. That left him only four. He had Saturdays and Sundays, of course, and on those two days he worked like a miner under a landslide. Augusta was not allowed to come on Saturday, though she was paid for that day. All the while that he was working so fiercely by night, he was earning his living during the day; carrying full university work and feeding himself out to hundreds of students in lectures and consultations. But that was another life.

St. Peter had managed for years to live two lives, both of them very intense. He would willingly have cut down on his university work, would willingly have given his students chaff and sawdust—many instructors had nothing else to give them and got on very well—but his misfortune was that he loved youth—he was weak to it, it kindled him. If there was one eager eye, one doubting, critical mind, one lively curiosity in a whole lecture-room full of commonplace boys and girls, he was its servant. That ardour could command him. It hadn't worn out with years, this responsiveness, any more than the magnetic currents wear out; it had nothing to do with Time.

But he had burned his candle at both ends to some purpose—he had got what he wanted. By many petty economies of purse, he had managed to be extravagant with not a cent in the world but his professor's salary— he didn't, of course, touch his wife's small income from her father. By eliminations and combinations so many and subtle that it now made his head ache to think of them, he had done full justice to his university lectures, and at the same time carried on an engrossing piece of creative work. A man can do anything if he wishes to enough, St. Peter believed. Desire is creation, is the magical element in that process. If there were an instrument by which to measure desire, one could foretell achievement. He had been able to measure it, roughly, just once, in his student Tom Outland,—and he had foretold.

There was one fine thing about this room that had been the scene of so many defeats and triumphs. From the window he could see, far away, just on the horizon, a long, blue, hazy smear—Lake Michigan, the inland sea of his childhood. Whenever he was tired and dull, when the white pages before him remained blank or were full of scratched-out sentences, then he left his desk, took the train to a little station twelve miles away, and spent a day on the lake with his sail-boat; jumping out to swim, floating on his back alongside, then climbing into his boat again.

When he remembered his childhood, he remembered blue water. There were certain human figures against it, of course; his practical, strong-willed Methodist mother, his gentle, weaned-away Catholic father, the old Kanuck grandfather, various brothers and sisters. But the great fact in life, the always possible escape from dullness, was the lake. The sun rose out of it, the day began there; it was like an open door that nobody could shut. The land and all its dreariness could never close in on you. You had only to look at the lake, and you knew you would soon be free. It was the first thing one saw in the morning, across the rugged cow pasture studded with shaggy pines, and it ran through the days like the weather, not a thing thought about, but a part of consciousness itself. When the ice chunks came in of a winter morning, crumbly and white, throwing off gold and rose-coloured reflections from a copper-coloured sun behind the grey clouds, he didn't observe the detail or know what it was that made him happy; but now, forty years later, he could recall all its aspects perfectly. They had made pictures in him when he was unwilling and unconscious, when his eyes were merely open wide.

When he was eight years old, his parents sold the lakeside farm and dragged him and his brothers and sisters out to the wheat lands of central Kansas. St. Peter nearly died of it. Never could he forget the few moments on the train when that sudden, innocent blue across the sand dunes was dying for ever from his sight. It was like sinking for the third time. No later anguish, and he had had his share, went so deep or seemed so final. Even in his long, happy student years with the Thierault family in France, that stretch of blue water was the one thing he was home-sick for. In the summer he used to go with the Thierault boys to Brittany or to the Languedoc coast; but his lake was itself, as the Channel and the Mediterranean were themselves. "No," he used to tell the boys, who were always asking him about *le Michigan,* "it is altogether different. It is a sea, and yet it is not salt. It is blue, but quite another blue. Yes, there are clouds and mists and sea-gulls, but— I don't know, *il est toujours plus naïf.*"

Afterward, when St. Peter was looking for a professorship, because he was very much in love and must marry at once, out of the several positions offered him he took the one at Hamilton, not because it was the best, but because it seemed to him that any place near the lake was a place where one could live. The sight of it from his study window these many years had been of more assistance than all the convenient things he had done without would have been.

Just in that corner, under Augusta's archaic "forms," he had always meant to put the filing-cabinets he had never spared the time or money to buy. They would have held all his notes and pamphlets, and the spasmodic rough drafts of passages far ahead. But he had never got them, and now he really didn't need them; it would be like locking the stable after the horse is stolen. For the horse was gone—that was the thing he was feeling most just now. In spite of all he'd neglected, he had completed his *Spanish Adventurers* in eight volumes—without filing-cabinets or money or a decent study or a decent stove—and without encouragement, Heaven knew! For all the interest the first three volumes awoke in the world, he might as well have dropped them into Lake Michigan. They had been timidly reviewed by other professors of history, in technical and educational journals. Nobody saw that he was trying to do something quite different—they merely thought he was trying to do the usual thing, and had not succeeded very well. They recommended to him the more even and genial style of John Fiske.

St. Peter hadn't, he could honestly say, cared a

whoop—not in those golden days. When the whole plan of his narrative was coming clearer and clearer all the time, when he could feel his hand growing easier with his material, when all the foolish conventions about that kind of writing were falling away and his relation with his work was becoming every day more simple, natural, and happy,—he cared as little as the Spanish Adventurers themselves what Professor So-and-So thought about them. With the fourth volume he began to be aware that a few young men, scattered about the United States and England, were intensely interested in his experiment. With the fifth and sixth, they began to express their interest in lectures and in print. The two last volumes brought him a certain international reputation and what were called rewards—among them, the Oxford prize for history, with its five thousand pounds, which had built him the new house into which he did not want to move.

"Godfrey," his wife had gravely said one day, when she detected an ironical turn in some remark he made about the new house, "is there something you would rather have done with that money than to have built a house with it?"

"Nothing, my dear, nothing. If with that cheque I could have bought back the fun I had writing my history, you'd never have got your house. But one couldn't get that for twenty thousand dollars. The great pleasures don't come so cheap. There is nothing else, thank you."

That evening St. Peter was in the new house, dressing for dinner. His two daughters and their husbands were dining with them, also an English visitor. Mrs. St. Peter heard the shower going as she passed his door. She entered his room and waited until he came out in his bath-robe, rubbing his wet, ink-black hair with a towel.

"Surely you'll admit that you like having your own bath," she said, looking past him into the glittering white cubicle, flooded with electric light, which he had just quitted.

"Whoever said I didn't? But more than anything else, I like my closets. I like having room for all my clothes, without hanging one coat on top of another, and not having to get down on my marrow-bones and fumble in dark corners to find my shoes."

"Of course you do. And it's much more dignified, at your age, to have a room of your own."

"It's convenient, certainly, though I hope I'm not so old as to be personally repulsive?" He glanced into the mirror and straightened his shoulders as if he were trying on a coat.

Mrs. St. Peter laughed,—a pleasant, easy laugh with genuine amusement in it. "No, you are very handsome, my dear, especially in your bath-robe. You grow better-looking and more intolerant all the time."

"Intolerant?" He put down his shoe and looked up

at her. The thing that stuck in his mind constantly was that she was growing more and more intolerant, about everything except her sons-in-law; that she would probably continue to do so, and that he must school himself to bear it.

"I suppose it's a natural process," she went on, "but you ought to try, try seriously, I mean, to curb it where it affects the happiness of your daughters. You are too severe with Scott and Louie. All young men have foolish vanities—you had plenty."

St. Peter sat with his elbows on his knees, leaning forward and playing absently with the tassels of his bath-robe. "Why, Lillian, I have exercised the virtue of patience with those two young men more than with all the thousands of young ruffians who have gone through my class-rooms. My forbearance is overstrained, it's gone flat. That's what's the matter with me."

"Oh, Godfrey, how can you be such a poor judge of your own behaviour? But we won't argue about it now. You'll put on your dinner coat? And do try to be sympathetic and agreeable to-night."

Half an hour later Mr. and Mrs. Scott McGregor and Mr. and Mrs. Louie Marsellus arrived, and soon after them the English scholar, Sir Edgar Spilling, so anxious to do the usual thing in America that he wore a morning street suit. He was a gaunt, rugged, large-boned man of fifty, with long legs and arms, a pear-shaped face, and a drooping, pre-war moustache. His specialty was Spanish history, and he had come all the way to

Hamilton, from his cousin's place in Saskatchewan, to enquire about some of Doctor St. Peter's "sources."

Introductions over, it was the Professor's son-in-law, Louie Marsellus, who took Sir Edgar in hand. He remembered having met in China a Walter Spilling, who was, it turned out, a brother of Sir Edgar. Marsellus had also a brother there, engaged in the silk trade. They exchanged opinions on conditions in the Orient, while young McGregor put on his horn-rimmed spectacles and roamed restlessly up and down the library. The two daughters sat near their mother, listening to the talk about China.

Mrs. St. Peter was very fair, pink and gold,—a pale gold, now that she was becoming a little grey. The tints of her face and hair and lashes were so soft that one did not realize, on first meeting her, how very definitely and decidedly her features were cut, under the smiling infusion of colour. When she was annoyed or tired, the lines became severe. Rosamond, the elder daughter, resembled her mother in feature, though her face was heavier. Her colouring was altogether different; dusky black hair, deep dark eyes, a soft white skin with rich brunette red in her cheeks and lips. Nearly everyone considered Rosamond brilliantly beautiful. Her father, though he was very proud of her, demurred from the general opinion. He thought her too tall, with a rather awkward carriage. She stooped a trifle, and was wide in the hips and shoulders. She had, he sometimes remarked to her mother, exactly the wide femur and flat shoulder-blade of his old slab-sided Kanuck grandfather. For a tree-hewer they were an asset. But St. Peter was very critical. Most people saw only Rosamond's smooth black head and white throat, and the red of her curved lips that was like the duskiness of dark, heavy-scented roses.

Kathleen, the younger daughter, looked even younger than she was—had the slender, undeveloped figure then very much in vogue. She was pale, with light hazel eyes, and her hair was hazel-coloured with distinctly green glints in it. To her father there was something very charming in the curious shadows her wide cheekbones cast over her cheeks, and in the spirited tilt of her head. Her figure in profile, he used to tell her, looked just like an interrogation point.

Mrs. St. Peter frankly liked having a son-in-law who could tot up acquaintances with Sir Edgar from the Soudan to Alaska. Scott, she saw, was going to be sulky because Sir Edgar and Marsellus were talking about things beyond his little circle of interests. She made no effort to draw him into the conversation, but let him prowl like a restless leopard among the books. The Professor was amiable, but quiet. When the second maid came to the door and signalled that dinner was ready—dinner was signalled, not announced—Mrs. St. Peter took Sir Edgar and guided him to his seat at her right, while the others found their usual places. After they had finished the soup, she had some difficulty in summoning the little maid to take away the plates, and explained to her guest that the electric bell, under the table, wasn't connected as yet—they had been in the new house less than a week, and the trials of building were not over.

"Oh? Then if I had happened along a fortnight ago I shouldn't have found you here? But it must be very interesting, building your own house and arranging it as you like," he responded.

Marsellus, silenced during the soup, came in with a warm smile and a slight shrug of the shoulders. "Building is the word with us, Sir Edgar, my—oh, isn't it! My wife and I are in the throes of it. We are building a country house, rather an ambitious affair, out on the wooded shores of Lake Michigan. Perhaps you would like to run out in my car and see it? What are your engagements for to-morrow? I can take you out in half an hour, and we can lunch at the Country Club. We have a magnificent site; primeval forest behind us and the lake in front, with our own beach—my father-in-law, you must know, is a formidable swimmer. We've been singularly fortunate in our architect,—a young Norwegian, trained in Paris. He's doing us a Norwegian manor house, very harmonious with its setting, just the right thing for rugged pine woods and high headlands."

Sir Edgar seemed most willing to make this excursion, and allowed Marsellus to fix an hour, greatly to the surprise of McGregor, whose look at his wife implied that he entertained serious doubts whether this baronet with walrus moustaches amounted to much after all.

The engagement made, Louie turned to Mrs. St. Peter. "And won't you come too, Dearest? You haven't been out since we got our wonderful wrought-iron door fittings from Chicago. We found just the right sort of hinge and latch, Sir Edgar, and had all the others copied from it. None of your Colonial glass knobs for us!"

Mrs. St. Peter sighed. Scott and Kathleen had just glass-knobbed their new bungalow throughout, yet she knew Louie didn't mean to hurt their feelings—it was his heedless enthusiasm that made him often say untactful things.

"We've been extremely fortunate in getting all the little things right," Louie was gladly confiding to Sir Edgar. "There's really not a flaw in the conception. I can say that, because I'm a mere onlooker; the whole thing's been done by the Norwegian and my wife and Mrs. St. Peter. And," he put his hand down affectionately upon Mrs. St. Peter's bare arm, "*and* we've named our place! I've already ordered the house stationery. No, Rosamond, I won't keep our little secret any longer. It will please your father, as well as your mother. We call our place 'Outland,' Sir Edgar."

He dropped the announcement and drew back. His mother-in-law rose to it—Spilling could scarcely be expected to understand.

"How splendid, Louie! A real inspiration."

"Yes, isn't it? I knew that would go to your hearts."

29

The Professor had expressed his emotion only by lifting his heavy, sharply uptwisted eyebrows. "Let me explain, Sir Edgar," Marsellus went on eagerly. "We have named our place for Tom Outland, a brilliant young American scientist and inventor, who was killed in Flanders, fighting with the Foreign Legion, the second year of the war, when he was barely thirty years of age. Before he dashed off to the front, this youngster had discovered the principle of the Outland vacuum, worked out the construction of the Outland engine that is revolutionizing aviation. He not only invented it, but, curiously enough for such a hot-headed fellow, had taken pains to protect it by patent. He had no time to communicate his discovery or to commercialize it— simply bolted to the front and left the most important discovery of his time to take care of itself."

Sir Edgar, fork arrested, looked a trifle dazed. "Am I to understand that you are referring to the inventor of the Outland engine?"

Louie was delighted. "Exactly that! Of course you would know all about it. My wife was young Outland's fiancée—is virtually his widow. Before he went to France he made a will in her favour; he had no living relatives, indeed. Toward the close of the war we began to sense the importance of what Outland had been doing in his laboratory—I am an electrical engineer by profession. We called in the assistance of experts and got the idea over from the laboratory to the trade. The monetary returns have been and are, of course, large."

While Louie paused long enough to have some intercourse with the roast before it was taken away, Sir Edgar remarked that he himself had been in the Air Service during the war, in the construction department, and that it was most extraordinary to come thus by chance upon the genesis of the Outland engine.

"You see," Louie told him, "Outland got nothing out of it but death and glory. Naturally, we feel terribly indebted. We feel it's our first duty in life to use that money as he would have wished—we've endowed scholarships in his own university here, and that sort of thing. But our house we want to have as a sort of memorial to him. We are going to transfer his laboratory there, if the university will permit,—all the apparatus he worked with. We have a room for his library and pictures. When his brother scientists come to Hamilton to look him up, to get information about him, as they are doing now already, at Outland they will find his books and instruments, all the sources of his inspiration."

"Even Rosamond," murmured McGregor, his eyes upon his cool green salad. He was struggling with a desire to shout to the Britisher that Marsellus had never so much as seen Tom Outland, while he, McGregor, had been his classmate and friend.

Sir Edgar was as much interested as he was mystified. He had come here to talk about manuscripts shut up in certain mouldering monasteries in Spain, but he had almost forgotten them in the turn the conversation had taken. He was genuinely interested in aviation and all its problems. He asked few questions, and his comments were almost entirely limited to the single exclamation, "Oh!" But this, from his lips, could mean a great many things; indifference, sharp interrogation, sympathetic interest, the nervousness of a modest man on hearing disclosures of a delicately personal nature. McGregor, before the others had finished dessert, drew a big cigar from his pocket and lit it at one of the table candles, as the horridest thing he could think of to do.

When they left the dining-room, St. Peter, who had scarcely spoken during dinner, took Sir Edgar's arm and said to his wife: "If you will excuse us, my dear, we have some technical matters to discuss." Leading his guest into the library, he shut the door.

Marsellus looked distinctly disappointed. He stood gazing wistfully after them, like a little boy told to go to bed. Louie's eyes were vividly blue, like hot sapphires, but the rest of his face had little colour—he was a rather mackerel-tinted man. Only his eyes, and his quick, impetuous movements, gave out the zest for life with which he was always bubbling. There was nothing Semitic about his countenance except his nose—that took the lead. It was not at all an unpleasing feature, but it grew out of his face with masterful strength, well-rooted, like a vigorous oak-tree growing out of a hill-side.

Mrs. St. Peter, always concerned for Louie, asked him to come and look at the new rug in her bedroom.

This revived him; he took her arm, and they went upstairs together.

McGregor was left with the two sisters. "Outland, outlandish!" he muttered, while he fumbled about for an ash-tray. Rosamond pretended not to hear him, but the dusky red on her cheeks crept a little farther toward her ears.

"Remember, we are leaving early, Scott," said Kathleen. "You have to finish your editorial to-night."

"Surely you don't make him work at night, too?" Rosamond asked. "Doesn't he have to rest his brain sometimes? Humour is always better if it's spontaneous."

"Oh, that's the trouble with me," Scott assured her. "Unless I keep my nose to the grindstone, I'm too damned spontaneous and tell the truth, and the public won't stand for it. It's not an editorial I have to finish, it's the daily prose poem I do for the syndicate, for which I get twenty-five beans. This is the motif:

'When your pocket is under-moneyed and your fancy is over-girled, you'll have to admit while you're cursing it, it's a mighty darned good old world.'

Bang, bang!"

He threw his cigar-end savagely into the fireplace. He knew that Rosamond detested his editorials and his jingles. She had fastidious taste in literature, like her mother—though he didn't think she had half the general intelligence of his wife. She also, now that she was Tom Outland's heir, detested to hear sums of money mentioned, especially small sums.

After the good-nights were said, and they were outside the front door, McGregor seized his wife's elbow and rushed her down the walk to the gate where his Ford was parked, breaking out in her ear as they ran: "Now what the hell is a virtual widow? Does he mean a virtuous widow, or the reverseous? Bang, bang!"

THREE

St. Peter awoke the next morning with the wish that he could be transported on his mattress from the new house to the old. But it was Sunday, and on that day his wife always breakfasted with him. There was no way out; they would meet at compt.

When he reached the dining-room Lillian was already at the table, behind the percolator. "Good morning, Godfrey. I hope you had a good night." Her tone just faintly implied that he hadn't deserved one.

"Excellent. And you?"

"I had a good conscience." She smiled ruefully at him. "How can you let yourself be ungracious in your own house?"

"Oh, dear! And I went to sleep happy in the belief that I hadn't said anything amiss the whole evening."

"Nor anything aright, that I heard. Your disapproving silence can kill the life of any company."

"It didn't seem to, last night. You're entirely wrong about Marsellus. He doesn't notice."

"He's too polite to *take* notice, but he feels it. He's very sensitive, under a well-schooled impersonal manner."

St. Peter laughed. "Nonsense, Lillian! If he were, he couldn't pick up a dinner party and walk off with it, as he almost always does. I don't mind when it's our dinner, but I hate seeing him do it in other people's houses."

"Be fair, Godfrey. You know that if you'd once begun to talk about your work in Spain, Louie would have followed it up with enthusiasm. Nobody is prouder of you than he."

"That's why I kept quiet. Support can be too able—certainly too fluent."

"There you are; the dog in the manger! You won't let him discuss your affairs, and you are annoyed when he talks about his own."

"I admit I can't bear it when he talks about Outland as his affair. (I mean Tom, of course, not their confounded place!) This calling it after him passes my comprehension. And Rosamond's standing for it! It's brazen impudence."

Mrs. St. Peter frowned pensively. "I knew you wouldn't like it, but they were so pleased about it, and their motives are so generous——"

"Hang it, Outland doesn't need their generosity! They've got everything he ought to have had, and the least they can do is to be quiet about it, and not convert his very bones into a personal asset. It all comes down to this, my dear: one likes the florid style, or one doesn't. You yourself used not to like it. And will you give me some more coffee, please?"

She refilled his cup and handed it across the table. "Nice hands," he murmured, looking critically at them as he took it, "always such nice hands."

"Thank you. I dislike floridity when it is beaten up to cover the lack of something, to take the place of something. I never disliked it when it came from exuberance. Then it isn't floridness, it's merely strong colour."

"Very well; some people don't care for strong colour. It fatigues them." He folded his napkin. "Now I must be off to my desk."

"Not quite yet. You never have time to talk to me. Just when did it begin, Godfrey, in the history of manners—that convention that if a man were pleased with his wife or his house or his success, he shouldn't say so, frankly?" Mrs. St. Peter spoke thoughtfully, as if she had considered this matter before.

"Oh, it goes back a long way. I rather think it began in the Age of Chivalry—King Arthur's knights. Whoever it was lived in that time, some feeling grew up that a man should do fine deeds and not speak of them, and that he shouldn't speak the name of his lady, but sing of her as a Phyllis or a Nicolette. It's a nice idea, reserve about one's deepest feelings: keeps them fresh."

"The Oriental peoples didn't have an Age of Chivalry. They didn't need one," Lillian observed. "And this reserve—it becomes in itself ostentatious, a vain-glorious vanity."

"Oh, my dear, all is vanity! I don't dispute that. Now I must really go, and I wish I could play the game as well as you do. I have no enthusiasm for being a father-in-law. It's you who keep the ball rolling. I fully appreciate that."

"Perhaps," mused his wife, as he rose, "it's because you didn't get the son-in-law you wanted. And yet he was highly coloured, too."

The Professor made no reply to this. Lillian had been fiercely jealous of Tom Outland. As he left the house, he was reflecting that people who are intensely in love when they marry, and who go on being in love, always meet with something which suddenly or gradually makes a difference. Sometimes it is the children, or the grubbiness of being poor, sometimes a second infatuation. In their own case it had been, curiously enough, his pupil, Tom Outland.

St. Peter had met his wife in Paris, when he was but twenty-four, and studying for his doctorate. She too was studying there. French people thought her an English girl because of her gold hair and fair complexion. With her really radiant charm, she had a very interesting mind—but it was quite wrong to call it mind, the connotation was false. What she had was a richly endowed nature that responded strongly to life and art, and very vehement likes and dislikes which were often quite out of all proportion to the trivial object or person that aroused them. Before his marriage, and for years afterward, Lillian's prejudices, her divinations about people and art (always instinctive and unexplained, but nearly always right), were the most interesting things in St. Peter's life. When he accepted almost the first position offered him, in order to marry at once, and came to take the chair of European history at Hamilton, he was thrown upon his wife for mental companionship. Most of his colleagues were much older than he, but they were not his equals either in scholarship or in experience of the world. The only other man in the faculty who was carrying on important research work was Doctor Crane, the professor of physics. St. Peter saw a good deal of him, though outside his specialty he was uninteresting—a narrow-minded man, and painfully unattractive. Years ago Crane had begun to suffer from a malady which in time proved incurable, and which now sent him up for an operation periodically. St. Peter had had no friend in Hamilton of whom Lillian could possibly be jealous until Tom Outland came along, so well fitted by nature and early environment to help him with his work on the Spanish Adventurers.

When he had almost reached his old house and his study, the Professor remembered that he really must have an understanding with his landlord, or the place would be rented over his head. He turned and went down into another part of the city, by the car shops, where only workmen lived, and found his landlord's little toy house, set on a hillside, over a basement faced up with red brick and covered with hop vines. Old Appelhoff was sitting on a bench before his door, making a broom. Raising broom corn was one of his economies. Beside him was his dachshund bitch, Minna.

St. Peter explained that he wanted to stay on in the empty house, and would pay the full rent each month. So irregular a project annoyed Appelhoff. "I like fine to oblige you, Professor, but dey is several parties looking at de house already, an' I don't like to lose a year's rent for maybe a few months."

"Oh, that's all right, Fred. I'll take it for the year, to simplify matters. I want to finish my new book before I move."

Fred still looked uneasy. "I better see de insurance man, eh? It says for purposes of domestic dwelling."

"He won't object. Let's have a look at your garden. What a fine crop of apples and sickle pears you have!"

"I don't like dem trees what don't bear not'ing," said the old man with sly humour, remembering the Professor's glistening, barren shrubs and the good ground wasted behind his stucco wall.

"How about your linden-trees?"

"Oh, dem flowers is awful good for de headache!"

"You don't look as if you were subject to it, Fred."

"Not me, but my woman always had."

"Pretty lonesome without her, Appelhoff?"

"I miss her, Professor, but I ain't just lonesome." The old man rubbed his bristly chin. "My Minna here is most like a person, and den I got so many t'ings to t'ink about."

"Have you? Pleasant things, I hope?"

"Well, all kinds. When I was young, in de old country, I had it hard to git my wife at all, an' I never had time to t'ink. When I come to dis country I had to work so turrible hard on dat farm to make crops an' pay debts, dat I was like a horse. Now I have it easy, an' I take time to t'ink about all dem t'ings."

St. Peter laughed. "We all come to it, Appelhoff. That's one thing I'm renting your house for, to have room to think. Good morning."

Crossing the public park, on his way back to the old house, he espied his professional rival and enemy, Professor Horace Langtry, taking a Sunday morning stroll— very well got up in English clothes he had brought back from his customary summer in London, with a bowler hat of unusual block and a horn-handled walking-stick. In twenty years the two men had scarcely had speech with each other beyond a stiff "good morning." When Langtry first came to the university he looked hardly more than a boy, with curly brown hair and such a fresh complexion that the students called him Lily Langtry. His round pink cheeks and round eyes and round chin made him look rather like a baby grown big. All these years had made little difference, except that his curls were now quite grey, his rosy cheeks even rosier, and his mouth dropped a little at the corners, so that he looked like a baby suddenly grown old and rather cross about it.

Seeing St. Peter, the younger man turned abruptly into a side alley, but the Professor overtook him.

"Good morning, Langtry. These elms are becoming real trees at last. They've changed a good deal since we first came here."

Doctor Langtry moved his rosy chin sidewise over his high double collar. "Good morning, Doctor St. Peter. I really don't remember much about the trees. They seem to be doing well now."

St. Peter stepped abreast of him. "There have been many changes, Langtry, and not all of them are good. Don't you notice a great difference in the student body as a whole, in the new crop that comes along every year now—how different they are from the ones of our early years here?"

The smooth chin turned again, and the other professor of European history blinked. "In just what respect?"

"Oh, in the all-embracing respect of quality! We have hosts of students, but they're a common sort."

"Perhaps. I can't say I've noticed it." The air between the two colleagues was not thawing out any. A church-bell rang. Langtry started hopefully. "You must excuse me, Doctor St. Peter, I am on my way to service."

The Professor gave it up with a shrug. "All right, all right, Langtry, as you will. *Quelle folie!*"

Langtry half turned back, hesitated on the ball of his suddenly speeding foot, and said with faultless politeness: "I beg your pardon?"

St. Peter waved his hand with a gesture of negation,

and detained the church-goer no longer. He sauntered along slackly through the hot September sunshine, wondering why Langtry didn't see the absurdity of their long grudge. They had always been directly opposed in matters of university policy, until it had almost become a part of their professional duties to outwit and cramp each other.

When young Langtry first came there, his specialty was supposed to be American history. His uncle was president of the board of regents, and very influential in State politics; the institution had to look to him, indeed, to get its financial appropriations passed by the Legislature. Langtry was a Tory in his point of view, and was considered very English in his tone and manner. His lectures were dull, and the students didn't like him. Every inducement was offered to make his courses popular. Liberal credits were given for collateral reading. A student could read almost anything that had ever been written in the United States and get credit for it in American history. He could charge up the time spent in perusing "The Scarlet Letter" to Colonial history, and "Tom Sawyer" to the Missouri Compromise, it was said. St. Peter openly criticized these lax methods, both to the faculty and to the regents. Naturally, "Madame Langtry" paid him out. During the Professor's second Sabbatical year in Spain, Horace and his uncle together very nearly got his department away from him. They worked so quietly that it was only at the eleventh hour that St. Peter's old students throughout the State got wind of what was going on, dropped their various businesses and professions for a few days, and came up to the capital in dozens and saved his place for him. The opposition had been so formidable that when it came time for his third year away, the Professor had not dared ask for it, but had taken an extension of his summer vacation instead. The fact that he was carrying on another line of work than his lectures, and was publishing books that weren't strictly text-books, had been used against him by Langtry's uncle.

As Langtry felt that the unpopularity of his course was due to his subject, a new chair was created for him. There couldn't be two heads in European history, so the board of regents made for him a chair of Renaissance history, or, as St. Peter said, a Renaissance chair of history. Of late years, for reasons that had not much to do with his lectures, Langtry had prospered better. To the new generations of country and village boys now pouring into the university in such large numbers, Langtry had become, in a curious way, an instructor in manners,—what is called an "influence." To the football-playing farmer boy who had a good allowance but didn't know how to dress or what to say, Langtry looked like a short cut. He had several times taken parties of undergraduates to London for the summer, and they had come back wonderfully brushed up. He introduced a very popular fraternity into the university, and its members looked after his interests, as did its affiliated sorority. His standing on the faculty was now quite as good as St. Peter's own, and the Professor wondered what Langtry still had to be sore about.

What was the use of keeping up the feud? They had both come there young men, fighting for their places and their lives; now they were not very young any more; they would neither of them, probably, ever hold a better position. Couldn't Langtry see it was a draw, that they had both been beaten?

FOUR

On Monday afternoon St. Peter mounted to his study and lay down on the box-couch, tired out with his day at the university. The first few weeks of the year were very fatiguing for him; there were so many exhausting things besides his lectures and all the new students; long faculty meetings in which almost no one was ever frank, and always the old fight to keep up the standard of scholarship, to prevent the younger professors, who had a sharp eye to their own interests, from farming the whole institution out to athletics, and to the agricultural and commercial schools favoured and fostered by the State Legislature.

The September heat, too, was hard on him. He wanted to be out at the lake every day—it was never so fine as in late September. He was lying with closed eyes, resting his mind on the picture of intense autumn-blue water, when he heard a tap at the door and his daughter Rosamond entered, very handsome in a silk suit of a vivid shade of lilac, admirably suited to her complexion and showing that in the colour of her cheeks there was actually a tone of warm lavender. In that low room she seemed very tall indeed, a little out of drawing, as, to her father's eye, she so often did. Usually, however, people were aware only of her rich complexion, her curving, unresisting mouth and mysterious eyes. Tom Outland had seen nothing else, and he was a young man who saw a great deal.

"Am I interrupting something important, Papa?"

"No, not at all, my dear. Sit down."

On his writing-table she caught a glimpse of pages in a handwriting not his—a script she knew very well.

"Not much choice of chairs, is there?" she smiled. "Papa, I don't like to have you working in a place like this. It's not fitting."

"Much easier than to break in a new room, Rosie. A work-room should be like an old shoe; no matter how shabby, it's better than a new one."

"That's really what I came to see you about." Rosamond traced the edge of a hole in the matting with the tip of her lilac sunshade. "Won't you let me build you a little study in the back yard of the new house? I have such good ideas for it, and you would have no bother about it at all."

"Oh, thank you, Rosamond. It's most awfully nice of you to think of it. But keep it just an idea—it's better so. Lots of things are. For the present I'll plod on here. It's absurd, but it suits me. Habit is such a big part of work."

"With Augusta's old things lying about, and those dusty old forms? Why didn't she at least get those out of your way?"

"Oh, they have a right here, by long tenure. It's their room, too. I don't want to come upon them lying in some dump-heap on the road to the lake. They remind me of the times when you were little girls, and your first party frocks used to hang on them at night, when I worked."

Rosamond smiled, unconvinced. "Papa, don't joke with me. I've come to talk about something serious, and it's very difficult. You know I'm a little afraid of you." She dropped her shadowy, bewitching eyes.

"Afraid of me? Never!"

"Oh, yes, I am when you're sarcastic. You mustn't be to-day, please. Louie and I have often talked this over. We feel strongly about it. He's often been on the point of blurting out with it, but I've curbed him. You don't always approve of Louie and me. Of course it was only Louie's energy and technical knowledge that ever made Tom's discovery succeed commercially, but we don't feel that we ought to have all the returns from it. We think you ought to let us settle an income on you, so that you could give up your university work and devote all your time to writing and research. That is what Tom would have wanted."

St. Peter rose quickly, with the light, supple spring he had when he was very nervous, crossed to the window, wide on its hook, and half closed it. "My dear daughter," he said decisively, when he had turned round to her, "I couldn't possibly take any of Outland's money."

"But why not? You were the best friend he had in the world, he owed more to you than to anyone else, and he hated having you hampered by teaching. He admired your mind, and nothing would have pleased him more than helping you to do the work you do better than anyone else. If he were alive, that would be one of the first things he would use this money for."

"But he is not alive, and there was no word about me in his will, and so there is nothing to build your pretty theory upon. It's wonderfully nice of you and Louie, and I'm very pleased, you know."

"But Tom was so impractical, Father. He never thought it would mean more than a liberal dress allowance for me, if he thought at all. I don't know—he never spoke to me about it."

St. Peter smiled quizzically. "I'm not so sure about his impracticalness. When he was working on that gas, he once remarked to me that there might be a fortune in it. To be sure, he didn't wait to find out whether there was a fortune, but that had to do with quite another side of him. Yes, I think he knew his idea would make money and he wanted you to have it, with him or without him."

The young woman's face grew troubled. "Even if I married?"

"He wanted you to have whatever would make you happy."

She sighed luxuriously. "Louie has done that. The only thing that troubles me is, I feel you ought to have some of this money, that he would wish it. He was so full of gratitude, felt that he owed you so much."

Her father again rose, with that guarded, nervous movement. "Once and for all, Rosamond, understand that he owed me no more than I owed him. Nothing hurts me so much as to have any member of my family talk as if we had done something fine for that young man, brought him out, produced him. In a lifetime of teaching, I've encountered just one remarkable mind; but for that, I'd consider my good years largely wasted. And there can be no question of money between me and Tom Outland. I can't explain just how I feel about it, but it would somehow damage my recollections of him, would make that episode in my life commonplace like everything else. And that would be a great loss to me. I'm purely selfish in refusing your offer; my friendship with Outland is the one thing I will not have translated into the vulgar tongue."

His daughter looked perplexed and a little resentful.

"Sometimes," she murmured, "I think you feel I oughtn't to have taken it, either."

"You had no choice. For you it was settled by his own hand. Your bond with him was social, and it follows the laws of society, and they are based on property. Mine wasn't, and there was no material clause in it. He empowered you to carry out all his wishes, and I realize that you have responsibilities—but none toward me. There is Rodney Blake, of course, if he should ever turn up. You keep up some search for him?"

"Louie attends to it. He has investigated and rejected several impostors."

"Then, of course, there are other friends of Tom's. The Cranes, for instance?"

Rosamond's face grew hard. "I won't bother you about the Cranes, Papa. We will attend to them. Mrs. Crane is a common creature, and she is advised by that dreadful shyster brother of hers, Homer Bright. You know what he is."

"Oh, yes! He was about the greatest bluffer I ever had in my classes."

Rosamond had risen to go. "I want you to be awfully happy, daughter," St. Peter went on, "and Tom did. It's only young people like you and Louie who can get any fun out of money. And there is enough to cover the fine, the almost imaginary obligations. You won't be sorry if you are generous with people like the Cranes."

"Thank you, Papa. I shan't forget." Rosamond went down the narrow stairway, leaving behind her a faint, fresh odour of lavender and orrisroot, and her father lay down again on the box-couch. "A hint about the Cranes will be enough," he was thinking.

He didn't in the least understand his older daughter. Not that he pretended to understand Kathleen, either; but he usually knew how she would feel about things, and she had always seemed to need his protection more than Rosamond. When she was a student at the university, he used sometimes to see her crossing the campus alone, her head and shoulders lowered against the wind, her muff beside her face, her narrow skirt clinging close. There was something too plucky, too "I can-go-it-alone," about her quick step and jaunty little head; he didn't like it, it gave him a sudden pang. He would always call to her and catch up with her, and make her take his arm and be docile.

She had been much quicker at her lessons than Rosie, and very clever at water-colour portrait sketches. She had done several really good likenesses of her father—one, at least, was the man himself. With her mother she had no luck. She tried again and again, but the face was always hard, the upper lip longer than it seemed in life, the nose long and severe, and she made something cold and plaster-like of Lillian's beautiful complexion. "No, I don't see Mamma like that," she used to say, throwing out her chin. "Of course I don't! It just *comes* like that." She had done many heads of her sister, all very sentimental and curiously false, though Louie Marsellus protested to like them. Her drawing-teacher at the university had urged Kathleen to go to Chicago and study in the life classes at the Art Institute, but she said resolutely: "No, I can't really do anybody but Papa, and I can't make a living painting him."

"The only unusual thing about Kitty," her father used to tell his friends, "is that she doesn't think herself a bit unusual. Nowadays the girls in my classes who have a spark of aptitude for anything seem to think themselves remarkable."

Though wilfulness was implied in the line of her

figure, in the way she sometimes threw out her chin, Kathleen had never been deaf to reasoning, deaf to her father, but once; and that was when, shortly after Rosamond's engagement to Tom, she announced that she was going to marry Scott McGregor. Scott was young, was just getting a start as a journalist, and his salary was not large enough for two people to live upon. That fact, the St. Peters thought, would act as a brake upon the impetuous young couple. But soon after they were engaged Scott began to do his daily prose poem for a newspaper syndicate. It was a success from the start, and increased his earnings enough to enable him to marry. The Professor had expected a better match for Kitty. He was no snob, and he liked Scott and trusted him; but he knew that Scott had a usual sort of mind, and Kitty had flashes of something quite different. Her father thought a more interesting man would make her happier. There was no holding her back, however, and the curious part of it was that, after the very first, her mother supported her. St. Peter had a vague suspicion that this was somehow on Rosamond's account more than on Kathleen's; Lillian always worked things out for Rosamond. Yet at the time he couldn't see how Kathleen's marriage would benefit Rosie. "Rosie is like your second self," he once declared to his wife, "but you never pampered yourself at her age as you do her."

It was an intense September noon—warm, windy, golden, with the smell of ripe grapes and drying vines in the air, and the lake rolling blue on the horizon. Scott McGregor, going into the west corner of the university campus, caught sight of Mrs. St. Peter, just ahead of him, walking in the same direction. He ran and caught up with her.

"Hello, Lillian! Going in to see the Professor? So am I. I want him to go swimming with me—I'm cutting work. Shall we drop in and hear the end of his lecture, or sit down here on a bench in the sun?"

"We can go quietly to the door and listen. If it's not interesting, we can come back and sit down for a chat."

"Good! I came early to overhear a bit. This is the hour he's with his seniors, isn't it?"

They entered and went along the hall until they came to number 17; the door was ajar, and at the moment one of the students was speaking. When he finished, they heard the Professor reply to him.

"No, Miller, I don't myself think much of science as a phase of human development. It has given us a lot of ingenious toys; they take our attention away from the real problems, of course, and since the problems are insoluble, I suppose we ought to be grateful for distraction. But the fact is, the human mind, the individual mind, has always been made more interesting by dwelling on the old riddles, even if it makes nothing of them. Science hasn't given us any new amazements, except of the superficial kind we get from witnessing dexterity and sleight-of-hand. It hasn't given us any richer pleasures, as the Renaissance did, nor any new sins—not one! Indeed, it takes our old ones away. It's the laboratory, not the Lamb of God, that taketh away the sins of the world. You'll agree there is not much thrill about a physiological sin. We were better off when even the prosaic matter of taking nourishment could have the magnificence of a sin. I don't think you help people by making their conduct of no importance—you impoverish them. As long as every man and woman who crowded into the cathedrals on Easter Sunday was a principal in a gorgeous drama with God, glittering angels on one side and the shadows of evil coming and going on the other, life was a rich thing. The king and the beggar had the same chance at miracles and great temptations and revelations. And that's what makes men happy, believing in the mystery and importance of their own little individual lives. It makes us happy to surround our creature needs and bodily instincts with as much pomp and circumstance as possible. Art and religion (they are the same thing, in the end, of course) have given man the only happiness he has ever had.

"Moses learned the importance of that in the Egyptian court, and when he wanted to make a population of slaves into an independent people in the shortest possible time, he invented elaborate ceremonials to give them a feeling of dignity and purpose. Every act had some imaginative end. The cutting of the finger nails was a religious observance. The Christian theologians went over the books of the Law, like great artists, getting splendid effects by excision. They reset the stage with more space and mystery, throwing all the light upon a few sins of great dramatic value—only seven, you remember, and of those only three that are perpetually enthralling. With the theologians came the cathedral-builders; the sculptors and glass-workers and painters. They might, without sacrilege, have changed the prayer a little and said, *Thy will be done in art, as it is in heaven.* How can it be done anywhere else *as* it is in heaven? But I think the hour is up. You might tell me next week, Miller, what you think science has done for us, besides making us very comfortable."

As the young men filed out of the room, Mrs. St. Peter and McGregor went in.

"I came over to get you to go to the electrician's with me, Godfrey, but I won't make you. Scott wants you to run out to the lake, and it's such a fine day, you really should go."

"Car's outside. We'll just drop Lillian at the house, Doctor, and you can pick up your bathing-suit. We heard part of your lecture, by the way. How you get by the Methodists is still a mystery to me."

"I wish he would get into trouble, Scott," said Lillian as they left the building. "I wish he wouldn't talk to those fat-faced boys as if they were intelligent beings.

You cheapen yourself, Godfrey. It makes me a little ashamed."

"I was rather rambling on to-day. I'm sorry you happened along. There's a fellow in that lot, Tod Miller, who isn't slow, and he excites me to controversy."

"All the same," murmured his wife, "it's hardly dignified to think aloud in such company. It's in rather bad taste."

"Thank you for the tip, Lillian. I won't do it again."

It took Scott only twenty minutes to get out to the lake. He drew up at the bit of beach St. Peter had bought for himself years before; a little triangle of sand running out into the water, with a bath-house and seven shaggy pine-trees on it. Scott had to fuss with the car, and the Professor was undressed and in the water before him.

When McGregor was ready to go in, his father-in-law was some distance out, swimming with an overarm stroke, his head and shoulders well out of the water. He wore on his head a rubber visor of a kind he always brought home from France in great numbers. This one was vermilion, and was like a continuation of his flesh—his arms and back were burned a deep terracotta from a summer in the lake. His head and powerful reaching arms made a strong red pattern against the purple blue of the water. The visor was picturesque—his head looked sheathed and small and intensely alive, like the heads of the warriors on the Parthenon frieze in their tight, archaic helmets.

By five o'clock St. Peter and McGregor were dressed and lying on the sand, their overcoats wrapped about them, smoking. Suddenly Scott began to chuckle.

"Oh, Professor, you know your English friend, Sir Edgar Spilling? The day after I met him at your house, he came up to my office at the *Herald* to get some facts you'd been too modest to give him. When he was leaving he stood and looked at one of these motto cards I have over my desk, DON'T KNOCK, and said: 'May I ask why you don't have that notice on the outside of your door? I didn't observe any other way of getting in.' They never get wise, do they? He really went out to see Marsellus' place—seemed interested. Doctor, are you going to let them call that place after Tom?"

"My dear boy, how can I prevent it?"

"Well, you surely don't like the idea, do you?"

The Professor lit another cigarette and was a long while about it. When he had got it going, he turned on his elbow and looked at McGregor. "Scott, you must see that I can't make suggestions to Louie. He's perfectly consistent. He's a great deal more generous and public-spirited than I am, and my preferences would be enigmatical to him. I can't, either, very gracefully express myself to you about his affairs."

"I get you. Sorry he riles me so. I always say it shan't occur the next time, but it does." Scott took out his pipe and lay silent for a time, looking at the gold glow burning on the water and on the wings of the gulls as they flew by. His expression was wistful, rather mournful. He was a good-looking fellow, with sunburned blond hair, splendid teeth, attractive eyes that usually frowned a little unless he was laughing outright, a small, prettily cut mouth, restless at the corners. There was something moody and discontented about his face. The Professor had a great deal of sympathy for him; Scott was too good for his work. He had been delighted when his daily poem and his "uplift" editorials first proved successful, because that enabled him to marry. Now he could sell as many good-cheer articles as he had time to write, on any subject, and he loathed doing them. Scott had early picked himself out to do something very fine, and he felt that he was wasting his life and his talents. The new group of poets made him angry. When a new novel was discussed seriously by his friends, he was perfectly miserable. St. Peter knew that the poor boy had seasons of desperate unhappiness. His disappointed vanity ate away at his vitals like the Spartan boy's wolf, and only the deep lines in his young forehead and the twitching at the corners of his mouth showed that he suffered.

Not long ago, when the students were giving an historical pageant to commemorate the deeds of an early French explorer among the Great Lakes, they asked St. Peter to do a picture for them, and he had arranged one which amused him very much, though it had nothing to do with the subject. He posed his two sons-in-law in a tapestry-hung tent, for a conference between Richard Plantagenet and the Saladin, before the walls of Jerusalem. Marsellus, in a green dressing-gown and turban, was seated at a table with a chart, his hands extended in reasonable, patient argument. The Plantagenet was standing, his plumed helmet in his hand, his square yellow head haughtily erect, his unthoughtful brows fiercely frowning, his lips curled and his fresh face full of arrogance. The tableau had received no special notice, and Mrs. St. Peter had said dryly that she was afraid nobody saw his little joke. But the Professor liked his picture, and he thought it quite fair to both the young men.

The Professor happened to come home earlier than usual one bright October afternoon. He left the walk and cut across the turf, intending to enter by the open French window, but he paused a moment outside to admire the scene within. The drawing-room was full of autumn flowers, dahlias and wild asters and goldenrod. The red-gold sunlight lay in bright puddles on the thick blue carpet, made hazy aureoles about the stuffed blue chairs. There was, in the room, as he looked through the window, a rich, intense effect of autumn, something that presented October much more sharply and sweetly to him than the coloured maples and the aster-bordered paths by which he had come home. It struck him that the seasons sometimes gain by being brought into the house, just as they gain by being brought into painting, and into poetry. The hand, fastidious and bold, which selected and placed—it was that which made the difference. In Nature there is no selection.

In a corner, beside the steaming brass tea-kettle, sat Lillian and Louie, a little lacquer table between them, bending, it seemed, over a casket of jewels. Lillian held up lovingly in her fingers a green-gold necklace, evidently an old one, without stones. "Of course emeralds would be beautiful, Louie, but they seem a little out of scale—to belong to a different scheme of life than any you and Rosamond can live here. You aren't, after all, outrageously rich. When would she wear them?"

"At home, Dearest, with me, at our own dinner-table at Outland! I like the idea of their being out of scale. I've never given her any jewels. I've waited all this time to give her these. To me, her name spells emeralds."

Mrs. St. Peter smiled, easily persuaded. "You'll never be able to keep them. You'll show them to her."

"Oh, no, I won't! They are to stay at the jeweller's, in Chicago, until we all go down for the birthday party. That's another secret we have to keep. We have such lots of them!" He bent over her hand and kissed it with warmth.

St. Peter swung in over the window rail. "That is always the cue for the husband to enter, isn't it? What's this about Chicago, Louie?"

He sat down, and Marsellus brought him some tea, lingering beside his chair. "It must be a secret from Rosie, but you see it happens that the date of your lecture engagement at the University of Chicago is co-incident with her birthday, so I have planned that we shall all go down together. And among other diversions, we shall attend your lectures."

The Professor's eyebrows rose. "Bus-man's holiday for the ladies, I should say."

"But not for me. Remember, I wasn't in your classes, like Scott and Outland. I'd give a good deal if I'd had the chance!" Louie said somewhat plaintively. "So you must make it up to me."

"Come if you wish. Lectures seem to me a rather grim treat, Louie."

"Not to me. With a wink of encouragement I'll go on to Boston with you next winter, when you give the Lowell lectures."

"Would you, really? Next year's a long way off. Now I must get clean. I've been working in my other-house garden, and I'm scarcely fit to have tea with a beautiful lady and a smartly dressed gentleman. What am I to do about that garden in the end, Lillian? Destroy it? Or leave it to the mercy of the next tenants?"

As he went upstairs he turned at the bend of the staircase and looked back at them, again bending over their little box. Mrs. St. Peter was wearing the white silk crêpe that had been the most successful of her summer dresses, and an orchid velvet ribbon about her shining hair. She wouldn't have made herself look quite so well if Louie hadn't been coming, he reflected. Or was it that he wouldn't have noticed it if Louie hadn't been there? A man long accustomed to admire his wife in general, seldom pauses to admire her in a particular gown or attitude, unless his attention is directed to her by the appreciative gaze of another man.

Lillian's coquetry with her sons-in-law amused him. He hadn't foreseen it, and he found it rather the most piquant and interesting thing about having married daughters. It had begun with Scott—the younger sister was married before the elder. St. Peter had thought that Scott McGregor was the sort of fellow Lillian al-

63

ways found tiresome. But no; within a few weeks after Kathleen's marriage, arch and confidential relations began to be evident between them. Even now, when Louie was so much in the foreground, and Scott was touchy and jealous, Lillian was very tactful and patient with him.

With Louie, Lillian seemed to be launching into a new career, and Godfrey began to think that he understood his own wife very little. He would have said that she would feel about Louie just as he did; would have cultivated him as a stranger in the town, because he was so unusual and exotic, but without in the least wishing to adopt anyone so foreign into the family circle. She had always been fastidious to an unreasonable degree about small niceties of deportment. She could never forgive poor Tom Outland for the angle at which he sometimes held a cigar in his mouth, or for the fact that he never learned to eat salad with ease. At the dinner-table, if Tom, forgetting himself in talk, sometimes dropped back into railroad lunch-counter ways and pushed his plate away from him when he had finished a course, Lillian's face would become positively cruel in its contempt. Irregularities of that sort put her all on edge. But Louie could hurry audibly through his soup, or kiss her resoundingly on the cheek at a faculty reception, and she seemed to like it.

Yes, with her sons-in-law she had begun the game of being a woman all over again. She dressed for them, planned for them, schemed in their interests. She had begun to entertain more than for years past—the new house made a plausible pretext—and to use her influence and charm in the little anxious social world of Hamilton. She was intensely interested in the success and happiness of these two young men, lived in their careers as she had once done in his. It was splendid, St. Peter told himself. She wasn't going to have to face a stretch of boredom between being a young woman and being a young grandmother. She was less intelligent and more sensible than he had thought her.

When Godfrey came downstairs ready for dinner, Louie was gone. He walked up to the chair where his wife was reading, and took her hand.

"My dear," he said quite delicately, "I wish you could keep Louie from letting his name go up for the Arts and Letters. It's not safe yet. He's not been here long enough. They're a fussy little bunch, and he ought to wait until they know him better."

"You mean someone will blackball him? Do you really think so? But the Country Club——"

"Yes, Lillian; the Country Club is a big affair, and needs money. The Arts and Letters is a little group of fellows, and, as I said, fussy."

"Scott belongs," said Mrs. St. Peter rebelliously. "Did he tell you?"

"No, he didn't, and I shall not tell you who did. But if you're tactful, you can save Louie's feelings."

Mrs. St. Peter closed her book without glancing down at it. A new interest shone in her eyes and made them look quite through and beyond her husband. "I must see what I can do with Scott," she murmured.

St. Peter turned away to hide a smile. An old student of his, a friend who belonged to "the Outland period," had told him laughingly that he was sure Scott would blackball Marsellus if his name ever came to the vote. "You know Scott is a kid in some things," the friend had said. "He's a little sore at Marsellus, and says a secret ballot is the only way he can ever get him where it wouldn't hurt Mrs. St. Peter."

While the Professor was eating his soup, he studied his wife's face in the candlelight. It had changed so much since he found her laughing with Louie, and especially since he had dropped the hint about the Arts and Letters. It had become, he thought, too hard for the orchid velvet in her hair. Her upper lip had grown longer, and stiffened as it always did when she encountered opposition.

"Well," he reflected, "it will be interesting to see what she can do with Scott. That will make rather a test case."

SEVEN

Early in November there was a picturesque snow-storm, and that day Kathleen telephoned her father at the university, asking him to stop on his way home in the afternoon and help her to decide upon some new furs. As he approached McGregor's spick-and-span bungalow at four o'clock, he saw Louie's Pierce-Arrow standing in front, with Ned, the chauffeur and gardener, in the driver's seat. Just then Rosamond came out of the bungalow alone, and down the path to the sidewalk, without seeing her father. He noticed a singularly haughty expression on her face; her brows drawn together over her nose. The curl of her lips was handsome, but terrifying. He observed also something he had not seen before—a coat of soft, purple-grey fur, that quite disguised the wide, slightly stooping shoulders he regretted in his truly beautiful daughter. He called to her, very much interested. "Wait a minute, Rosie. I've not seen that before. It's extraordinarily becoming." He stroked his daughter's sleeve with evident pleasure. "You know, these things with a kind of lurking purple and lavender in them are splendid for you. They make your colour prettier than ever. It's only lately you've begun to wear them. Louie's taste, I suppose?"

"Of course. He selects all my things for me," said Rosamond proudly.

"Well, he does a good job. He knows what's right for you." St. Peter continued to look her up and down with satisfaction. "And Kathleen is getting new furs. You were advising her?"

"She didn't mention it to me," Rosamond replied in a guarded voice.

"No? And what do you call this, what beast?" he asked ingenuously, again stroking the fur with his bare hand.

"It's *taupe*."

"Oh, moleskin!" He drew back a little. "Couldn't be better for your complexion. And is it warm?"

"Very warm—and so light."

"I see, I see!" He took Rosamond's arm and escorted her to her car. "Give Louie my compliments on his choice." The motor glided away—he wished he could escape as quickly and noiselessly, for he was a coward. But he had a feeling that Kathleen was watching him from behind the sash curtains. He went up to the door and made a long and thorough use of the foot-scraper before he tapped on the glass. Kathleen let him in. She was very pale; even her lips, which were always pink, like the inside of a white shell, were without colour. Neither of them mentioned the just-departed guest.

"Have you been out in the park, Kitty? This is a pretty little storm. Perhaps you'll walk over to the old house with me presently." He talked soothingly while he took off his coat and rubbers. "And now for the furs!"

Kathleen went slowly into her bedroom. She was gone a great while—perhaps ten actual minutes. When she came back, the rims of her eyes were red. She carried four large pasteboard boxes, tied together with twine. St. Peter sprang up, took the parcel, and began untying the string. He opened the first and pulled out a brown stole. "What is it, mink?"

"No, it's Hudson Bay sable."

"Very pretty." He put the collar round her neck and drew back to look at it. But after a sharp struggle Kathleen broke down. She threw off the fur and buried her face in a fresh handkerchief.

"I'm so sorry, Daddy, but it's no use to-day. I don't want any furs, really. She spoils everything for me."

"Oh, my dear, my dear, you hurt me terribly!" St. Peter put his hands tenderly on her soft hazel-coloured hair. "Face it squarely, Kitty; you must not, you cannot, be envious. It's self-destruction."

"I can't help it, Father. I *am* envious. I don't think I would be if she let me alone, but she comes here with her magnificence and takes the life out of all our poor little things. Everybody knows she's rich, why does she have to keep rubbing it in?"

"But, Kitty dear, you wouldn't have her go home and change her coat before coming to see you?"

"Oh, it's not that, Father, it's everything! You know

we were never jealous of each other at home. I was always proud of her good looks and good taste. It's not her clothes, it's a feeling she has inside her. When she comes toward me, I feel hate coming toward me, like a snake's hate!"

St. Peter wiped his moist forehead. He was suffering with her, as if she had been in physical anguish. "We can't, dear, we can't, in this world, let ourselves think of things—of comparisons—like that. We are all too susceptible to ugly suggestions. If Rosamond has a grievance, it's because you've been untactful about Louie."

"Even if I have, why should she be so revengeful? Does she think nobody else calls him a Jew? Does she think it's a secret? I don't mind being called a Gentile."

"It's all in the way it's done, you know, Kitty. And you've shown that you were a little bored with all their new things, now haven't you?"

"I've shown that I don't like the way she over-dresses, I suppose. I would never have believed that Rosie could do anything in such bad taste. While she is here among her old friends, she ought to dress like the rest of us."

"But doesn't she? It seems to me her things look about like yours."

"Oh, Father, you're so simple! And Mother is very careful not to enlighten you. We go to the Guild to sew for the Mission fund, and Rosie comes in in a handmade French frock that cost more than all our dresses put together."

"But if hers are no prettier, what does it matter how much they cost?" He was watching Kathleen fearfully. Her pale skin had taken on a greenish tinge—there was no doubt about it. He had never happened to see that change occur in a face before, and he had never realized to what an ugly, painful transformation the common phrase "green with envy" referred.

"Oh, foolish, they are prettier, though you may not see it. It's not just the clothes"—she looked at him intently, and her eyes, in their reddened rims, expanded and cleared. "It's everything. When we were at home, Rosamond was a kind of ideal to me. What she thought about anything, decided it for me. But she's entirely changed. She's become Louie. Indeed, she's worse than Louie. He and all this money have ruined her. Oh, Daddy, why didn't you and Professor Crane get to work and stop all this before it began? You were to blame. You knew that Tom had left something that was worth a lot, both of you. Why didn't you *do* something? You let it lie there in Crane's laboratory for this—this Marsellus to come along and exploit, until he almost thinks it's his own idea."

"Things might have turned out the same, anyway," her father protested. "Whatever the process earned was Rosamond's. I wasn't in the mood to struggle with manufacturers, I know nothing of such things. And Crane needs every ounce of his strength for his own experiments. He doesn't care about anything but the extent of space."

"He'd better have taken a few days off and saved his friend's reputation. Tom trusted him with everything. It's too foolish; that poor man being cut to pieces by surgeons all the time, and picking up the little that's left of himself and bothering about the limitations of space—much good they'll do him!"

St. Peter rose, took both of his daughter's hands, and stood laughing at her. "Come now! You have more brains than that, Kitty. It happens you do understand that whatever poor Crane can find out about space is more good to him than all the money the Marselluses will ever have. But are you implying that if Crane and I had developed Tom's discovery, we might have kept Rosie and her money in the family, for ourselves?"

Kathleen threw up her head. "Oh, I don't want her money!"

"Exactly; nor do I. And we mustn't behave as if we did want it. If you permit yourself to be envious of Rosie, you'll be very foolish, and very unhappy."

The Professor walked away across the snowy park with a tired step. He was heavy-hearted. For Kathleen he had a special kind of affection. Perhaps it was because he had had to take care of her for one whole summer when she was little. Just as Mrs. St. Peter was ready to start for Colorado with the children, the younger one developed whooping-cough and had to be left at home with her father. He had opportunity to observe all her ways. She was only six, but he found her a square-dealing, dependable little creature. They worked out a satisfactory plan of life together. She was to play in the garden all morning, and was not on any account to disturb him in his study. After lunch he would take her to the lake or the woods, or he would read to her at home. She took pride in keeping her part of the contract. One day when he came out of his study at noon, he found her sitting on the third floor stairs, just outside his door, with the arnica bottle in one hand and the fingers of the other puffed up like wee pink sausages. A bee had stung her in the garden, and she had waited half the morning for sympathy. She was very independent, and would tug at her leggings or overshoes a great while before she asked for help.

When they were little girls, Kathleen adored her older sister and liked to wait on her, was always more excited about Rosie's new dresses and winter coat than about her own. This attachment had lasted even after they were grown. St. Peter had never seen any change in it until Rosamond announced her engagement to Louie Marsellus. Then, all at once, Kathleen seemed to be done with her sister. Her father believed she couldn't forgive Rosie's forgetting Tom so quickly.

It was dark when the Professor got back to the old house and sat down at his writing-table. He would have an hour on his notes, he told himself, in spite of families and fortunes. And he had it. But when he looked up from his writing as the Angelus was ringing, two faces at once rose in the shadows outside the yellow circle of his lamp: the handsome face of his older daughter, surrounded by violet-dappled fur, with a cruel upper lip and scornful half-closed eyes, as she had approached her car that afternoon before she saw him; and Kathleen, her square little chin set so fiercely, her white cheeks actually becoming green under her swollen eyes. He couldn't believe it. He rose quickly and went to his one window, opened it wider, and stood looking at the dark clump of pine-trees that told where the Physics building stood. A sharp pain clutched his heart. Was it for this the light in Outland's laboratory used to burn so far into the night!

EIGHT

The following week St. Peter went to Chicago to give his lectures. He had engaged rooms for himself and Lillian at a quiet hotel near the university. The Marselluses went down by the same train, and they all alighted at the station together, in a raging snow-storm. The St. Peters were to have tea with Louie at the Blackstone, before going to their own quarters.

Tea was served in Louie's suite on the lake front, with a fine view of the falling snow from the windows. The Professor was in a genial mood; he was glad to be in a big city again, in a luxurious hotel, and especially pleased to be able to sit in comfort and watch the storm over the water.

"How snug you are here, Louie! This is really very nice," he said, turning back from the window when Rosamond called him.

Louie came and put both hands on St. Peter's shoulders, exclaiming delightedly: "And do you like these rooms, sir? Well, I'm glad, for they're yours! Rosie and I are farther down the corridor. Not a word! It's all arranged. You are our guests for this engagement. We won't have our great scholar staying off in some grimy place on the South side. We want him where we can keep an eye on him."

Louie was so warm with his plan that the Professor could only express satisfaction. "And our luggage?"

"It's on the way. I cancelled your reservations and did everything in order. Now have your tea, but not too much. You dine early; you have an engagement for to-night. You and Dearest are going to the opera——Oh, not with us! We have other fish to fry. You are going off alone."

"Very well, Louie! And what are they giving to-night?"

"*Mignon.* It will remind you of your student days in Paris."

"It will. I always had *abonnement* at the Opéra Comique, and *Mignon* came round frequently. It's one of my favourites."

"I thought so!" Louie kissed both the ladies, to express his satisfaction. The Professor had forgotten his scruples about accepting lavish hospitalities. He was really very glad to have windows on the lake, and not to have to go away to another hotel. After the Marselluses went to their own apartment, he remarked to his wife, while he unpacked his bag, that it was much more convenient to be on the same floor with Louie and Rosamond. "Much better than cabbing across Chicago to meet them all the time, isn't it?"

At eight o'clock he and his wife were in their places in the Auditorium. The overture brought a smile to his lips and a gracious mood to his heart. The music seemed extraordinarily fresh and genuine still. It might grow old-fashioned, he told himself, but never old, surely, while there was any youth left in men. It was an expression of youth,—that, and no more; with the sweetness and foolishness, the lingering accent, the heavy stresses—the delicacy, too—belonging to that time. After the entrance of the hero, Lillian leaned toward him and whispered: "Am I over-credulous? He looks to me exactly like the pictures of Goethe in his youth."

"So he does to me. He is certainly as tall as Goethe. I didn't know tenors were ever so tall. The *Mignon* seems young, too."

She was slender, at any rate, and very fragile beside the courtly *Wilhelm*. When she began her immortal song, one felt that she was right for the part, the pure lyric soprano that suits it best, and in her voice there was something fresh and delicate, like deep wood flowers. *"Connais-tu—le pays"*—it stirred one like the odours of early spring, recalled the time of sweet, impersonal emotions.

When the curtain fell on the first act, St. Peter turned to his wife. "A fine cast, don't you think? And the harps are very good. Except for the wood-winds, I should say it was as good as any performance I ever heard at the Comique."

"How it does make one think of Paris, and of so many half-forgotten things!" his wife murmured. It had been long since he had seen her face so relaxed and reflective and undetermined.

Through the next act he often glanced at her. Curious, how a young mood could return and soften a face. More than once he saw a starry moisture shine in her eyes. If she only knew how much more lovely she was when she wasn't doing her duty!

"My dear," he sighed when the lights were turned on and they both looked older, "it's been a mistake, our having a family and writing histories and getting middle-aged. We should have been picturesquely shipwrecked together when we were young."

"How often I've thought that!" she replied with a faint, melancholy smile.

"You? But you're so occupied with the future, you adapt yourself so readily," he murmured in astonishment.

"One must go on living, Godfrey. But it wasn't the children who came between us." There was something lonely and forgiving in her voice, something that spoke of an old wound, healed and hardened and hopeless.

"You, you too?" he breathed in amazement. He took up one of her gloves and began drawing it out through his fingers. She said nothing, but he saw her lip quiver, and she turned away and began looking at the house through the glasses. He likewise began to examine the audience. He wished he knew just how it seemed to her. He had been mistaken, he felt. The heart of another is a dark forest, always, no matter how close it has been to one's own. Presently the melting music of the tenor's last aria brought their eyes together in a smile not altogether sad.

That night, after he was in bed, among unaccustomed surroundings and a little wakeful, St. Peter still played with his idea of a picturesque shipwreck, and he cast about for the particular occasion he would have chosen for such a finale. Before he went to sleep he found the very day, but his wife was not in it. Indeed, nobody was in it but himself, and a weather-dried little sea captain from the Hautes-Pyrénées, half a dozen spry seamen, and a line of gleaming snow peaks, agonizingly high and sharp, along the southern coast of Spain.

Louie arranged the birthday dinner in the public dining-room of the hotel, and three of the Professor's colleagues dined with them on that occasion. Louie had gone out to the university to hear St. Peter lecture, had met some of the faculty, and immediately invited them to dinner. They accepted—when was a professor known to refuse a good dinner? Rosamond was presented with her emeralds, and, as St. Peter afterward observed to his wife, practically all the guests in the dining-room were participants in the happy event. Lillian was doubtless right when she told him that, all the same, his fellow professors went away from the Blackstone that night respecting Godfrey St. Peter more than they had ever done before, and if they had marriageable daughters, they were certainly envying him his luck.

"That," her husband replied, "is my chief objection to public magnificence; it seems to show everybody up in the worst possible light. I'm not finding fault with anyone but myself, understand. When I consented to occupy an apartment I couldn't afford, I let myself in for whatever might follow."

They got back to Hamilton in bitter weather. The lake winds were scourging the town, and Scott had laryngitis and was writing prose poems about the pleasures of tending your own furnace when the thermometer is twenty below.

"Godfrey," said Mrs. St. Peter when he set off for his class-room on the morning after their return, "surely you're not going to the old house this afternoon. It will be like a refrigerating-plant. There's no way of heating your study except by that miserable little stove."

"There never was, my dear. I got along a good many years."

"It was very different when the house below was heated. That stove isn't safe when you keep the window open. A gust of wind might blow it out at any moment, and if you were at work you'd never notice until you were half poisoned by gas. You'll get a fine headache one of these days."

"I've got headaches that way before, and survived them," he said stubbornly.

"How can you be so perverse? You know things are different now, and you ought to take more care of your health."

"Why so? It's not worth half so much as it was then."

His wife disregarded this. "And don't you think it's

a foolish extravagance to go on paying the rent of an entire house, in order to spend a few hours a day in one very uncomfortable room of it?"

The Professor's dark skin reddened, and the ends of his formidable eyebrows ascended toward his black hair. "It's almost my only extravagance," he muttered fiercely.

"How irritable and unreasonable he is becoming!" his wife reflected, as she heard him putting on his over-shoes in the hall.

For Christmas day the weather turned mild again. There would be a family dinner in the evening, but St. Peter was going to have the whole day to himself, in the old house. He asked his wife to put him up some sandwiches, so that he needn't come back for lunch. He kept a few bottles of sherry in his study, in the old chest under the forms. Fortunately he had brought back a great deal of it from his last trip to Spain. It wasn't foresight—Prohibition was then unthinkable—but a lucky accident. He had gone with his inn-keeper to an auction, and bought in a dozen dozens of a sherry that went very cheap. He came home by the City of Mexico and got the wine through without duty.

As he was crossing the park with his sandwiches, he met Augusta coming back from Mass.

"Are you still going to the old house, Professor?" she asked reproachfully, her face smiling at him between her stiff black fur collar and her stiff black hat.

"Oh, yes, Augusta, but it's not the same. I miss you. There are never any new dresses on my ladies in the evening now. Won't you come in sometime and deck them out, as a surprise for me? I like to see them looking smart."

Augusta laughed. "You are a funny man, Doctor St. Peter. If anyone else said the things you do to your classes, I'd be scandalized. But I always tell people you don't mean half you say."

"And how do you know what I say to my classes, may I ask?"

"Why, of course, they go out and talk about it when you say slighting things about the Church," she said gravely.

"But, really, Augusta, I don't think I ever do."

"Well, they take it that way. They are not as smart as you, and you ought to be careful."

"It doesn't matter. What they think to-day, they'll forget to-morrow." He was walking beside Augusta, with a slack, indifferent stride, very unlike the step he had when he was full of something. "That reminds me: I've been wanting to ask you a question. That passage in the service about the Mystical Rose, Lily of Zion, Tower of Ivory—is that the Magnificat?"

Augusta stopped and looked at him. "Why, Professor! Did you receive *no* religious instruction at all?"

"How could I, Augusta? My mother was a Methodist, there was no Catholic church in our town in Kansas, and I guess my father forgot his religion."

"That happens, in mixed marriages." Augusta spoke meaningly.

"Ah, yes, I suppose so. But tell me, what is the Magnificat, then?"

"The Magnificat begins, *My soul doth magnify the Lord;* you must know that."

"But I thought the Magnificat was about the Virgin?"

"Oh, no, Professor! The Blessed Virgin composed the Magnificat."

St. Peter became intensely interested. "Oh, she did?"

Augusta spoke gently, as if she were prompting him and did not wish to rebuke his ignorance too sharply. "Why, yes, just as soon as the angel had announced to her that she would be the mother of our Lord, the Blessed Virgin composed the Magnificat. I always think of you as knowing everything, Doctor St. Peter!"

"And you're always finding out how little I know. Well, you don't give me away. You are very discreet."

Their ways parted, and both went on more cheerful than when they met. The Professor climbed to his study feeling quite as though Augusta had been there and brightened it up for him. (Surely she had said that the Blessed Virgin sat down and composed the Magnificat!) Augusta had been with them often in the holiday season, back in the years when holidays were holidays indeed. He had grown to like the reminders of herself that she left in his work-room—especially the toilettes upon the figures. Sometimes she made those terrible women entirely plausible!

In the early years, no matter how hard he was working, he had always felt the sense of holiday, of a special warmth and fragrance in the air, steal up to his study from the house below. When he was writing his best, he was conscious of pretty little girls in fresh dresses—

of flowers and greens in the comfortable, shabby sitting-room—of his wife's good looks and good taste—even of a better dinner than usual under preparation down-stairs. All the while he had been working so fiercely at his eight big volumes, he was not insensible to the domestic drama that went on beneath him. His mind had played delightedly with all those incidents. Just as, when Queen Mathilde was doing the long tapestry now shown at Bayeux,—working her chronicle of the deeds of knights and heroes,—alongside the big pattern of dramatic action she and her women carried the little playful pattern of birds and beasts that are a story in themselves; so, to him, the most important chapters of his history were interwoven with personal memories.

On this Christmas morning, with that sense of the past in his mind, the Professor went mechanically to work, and the morning disappeared. Before he knew it was passing, the bells from Augusta's church across the park rang out and told him it was gone. He pushed back his papers and arranged his writing-table for lunch.

He had been working hard, he judged, because he was so hungry. He peered with interest into the basket his wife had given him—a wicker bag, it was, really, that he had once bought full of strawberries at Gibral-tar. Chicken sandwiches with lettuce leaves, red Cali-fornia grapes, and two shapely, long-necked russet pears. That would do very well; and Lillian had thoughtfully put in one of her best dinner napkins, knowing he hated ugly linen. From the chest he took out a round cheese, and a bottle of his wine, and began to polish a sherry glass.

While he was enjoying his lunch, he was thinking of certain holidays he had spent alone in Paris, when he was living at Versailles, with the Thieraults, as tutor to their boys. There was one All Souls' Day when he had gone into Paris by an early train and had a magnificent breakfast on the Rue de Vaugirard—not at Foyot's, he hadn't money enough in those days to put his nose inside the place. After breakfast he went out to walk in the soft rainfall. The sky was of such an intense silvery grey that all the grey stone buildings along the Rue St. Jacques and the Rue Sufflot came out in that silver shine stronger than in sunlight. The shop windows were shut; on the bleak ascent to the Pantheon there was not a spot of colour, nothing but wet, shiny, quick-silvery grey, accented by black crevices, and weather-worn bosses white as wood-ash. All at once, from somewhere behind the Pantheon itself, a man and woman, pushing a hand-cart, came into the empty street. The cart was full of pink dahlias, all exactly the same colour. The young man was fair and slight, with a pale face; the woman carried a baby. Both they and the wheels of their barrow were splashed with mud. They must have come from a good way in the country, and were a weary, anxious-looking pair. They stopped at a corner before the Pantheon and fearfully scanned the bleak, silvery, deserted streets. The man went into a bakery, and his wife began to spread out the flowers, which were done up in large bouquets with fresh green chestnut-leaves. Young St. Peter approached and asked the price.

"*Deux francs cinquante, Monsieur,*" she said with a kind of desperate courage.

He took a bunch and handed her a five-franc note. She had no change. Her husband, watching from the bakery, came running across with a loaf of bread under his arm.

"*Deux francs cinquante,*" she called to him as he came up. He put his hand into his pocket and fumbled.

"*Deux francs cinquante,*" she repeated with painful tension. The price agreed upon had probably been a franc or a franc fifty. The man counted out the change to the student and looked at his wife with admiration. St. Peter was so pleased with his flowers that it hadn't occurred to him to get more; but all his life he had regretted that he didn't buy two bunches, and push their fortunes a little further. He had never again found dahlias of such a beautiful colour, or so charmingly arranged with bright chestnut-leaves.

A moment later he was strolling down the hill, wondering to whom he could give his bouquet, when a pathetic procession filed past him through the rain. The girls of a charity school came walking two and two, in hideous dark uniforms and round felt hats without ribbon or bow, marshalled by four black-bonneted nuns. They were all looking down, all but one—the pretty one, naturally—and she was looking sidewise, directly at the student and his flowers. Their eyes met, she smiled, and just as he put out his hand with the bouquet, one of the sisters flapped up like a black crow and shut the girl's pretty face from him. She would have to pay for that smile, he was afraid. Godfrey spent his day in the Luxembourg Gardens and walked back to the Gare St. Lazare at evening with nothing but his return ticket in his pocket, very glad to get home to Versailles in time for the family dinner.

When he first went to live with the Thieraults, he had found Madame Thierault severe and exacting, stingy about his laundry and grudging about the cheese and fruit he ate for dinner. But in the end she was very kind to him; she never pampered him, but he could depend upon her. Her three sons had always been his dearest friends. Gaston, the one he loved best, was dead—killed in the Boxer uprising in China. But Pierre still lived at Versailles, and Charles had a business in Marseilles. When he was in France their homes were his. They were much closer to him than his own brothers. It was one summer when he was in France, with Lillian and the two little girls, that the idea of writing a work upon the early Spanish explorers first occurred to him, and he had turned at once to the Thieraults. After giving his wife enough money to finish the summer and get home, he took the little that was left and went down to Marseilles to talk over his project with Charles Thierault *fils,* whose mercantile house did a business with Spain in cork. Clearly St. Peter would have to be in Spain as much as possible for the next few years, and he would have to live there very cheaply. The Thieraults were always glad of a chance to help him. Not with money,—they were too French and too logical for that. But they would go to any amount of trouble and no inconsiderable expense to save him a few thousand francs.

That summer Charles kept him for three weeks in his oleander-buried house in the Prado, until his little brig, *L'Espoir,* sailed out of the new port with a cargo for Algeciras. The captain was from the Hautes-Pyrénées, and his spare crew were all Provençals, seamen trained in that hard school of the Gulf of Lyons. On the voyage everything seemed to feed the plan of the work that was forming in St. Peter's mind; the skipper, the old Catalan second mate, the sea itself. One day stood out above the others. All day long they were skirting the south coast of Spain; from the rose of dawn to the gold of sunset the ranges of the Sierra Nevadas towered on their right, snow peak after snow peak, high beyond the flight of fancy, gleaming like crystal and topaz. St. Peter lay looking up at them from a little boat riding low in the purple water, and the design of his book unfolded in the air above him, just as definitely as the mountain ranges themselves. And the design was sound. He had accepted it as inevitable, had never meddled with it, and it had seen him through.

It was late on Christmas afternoon when the Professor got back to the new house, but he was in such a happy frame of mind that he feared nothing, not even a family dinner. He quite looked forward to it, on the contrary. His wife heard him humming his favorite air from *Matrimonio Segreto* while he was dressing.

That evening the two daughters of the house arrived almost at the same moment. When Rosamond threw off her cloak in the hall, her father noticed that she was wearing her new necklace. Kathleen stood looking at it, and was evidently trying to find courage to say something about it, when Louie helped her by breaking in.

"And, Kitty, you haven't seen our jewels! What do you think? Just look at it."

"I was looking. It's too lovely!"

"It's very old, you see, the gold. What a work I had finding it! She doesn't like anything showy, you know, and she doesn't care about intrinsic values. It must be beautiful, first of all."

"Well, it is that, surely."

Louie walked up and down, admiring his wife. "She carries off things like that, doesn't she? And yet, you know, I like her in simple things, too." He dropped into reflection, just as if he were alone and talking to himself. "I always remember a little bracelet she wore the night I first met her. A turquoise set in silver, wasn't it? Yes, a turquoise set in dull silver. Have you it yet, Rosie?"

"I think so." There was a shade of displeasure in Rosamond's voice, and she turned back into the hall to look for something. "Where are the violets you brought for Mamma?"

Mrs. St. Peter came in, followed by the maid and the cocktails. Scott began the usual Prohibition lament.

"Why don't you journalists tell the truth about it in print?" Louie asked him. "It's a case where you could do something."

"And lose my job? Not much! This country's split in two, socially, and I don't know if it's ever coming together. It's not so hard on me, I can drink hard liquor. But you and the Professor like wine and fancy stuff."

"Oh, it's nothing to us! We're going to France for the summer," Louie put his arm round his wife and rubbed his cheek against hers, saying caressingly, "and drink Burgundy, Burgundy, Burgundy!"

"Please take me with you, Louie," Mrs. St. Peter pleaded, to distract him from his wife. Nothing made the McGregors so uncomfortable and so wrathful as the tender moments which sometimes overtook the Marselluses in public.

"We are going to take you, and Papa too. That's our plan. I take him for safety. If I travelled on the Continent alone with two such handsome women, it wouldn't be tolerated. There would be a trumped-up quarrel, and a stiletto, and then somebody would be a widow," turning again to his wife.

"Come here, Louie." Mrs. St. Peter beckoned him. "I have a confession to make. I'm afraid there's no dinner for you to-night."

"No dinner for me?"

"No. There's nothing either you or Godfrey will like. It's Scott's dinner to-night. Your tastes are so different, I can't compromise. And this is his, from the cream soup to the frozen pudding."

"But who said I didn't like cream soup and frozen pudding?" Louie held out his hands to show their guiltlessness. "And are there *haricots verts* in cream sauce? I thought so! And I like those, too. The truth is, Dearest," he stood before her and tapped her chin with his finger, "the truth is that I like all Scott's dinners, it's he who doesn't like mine! He's the intolerant one."

"True for you, Louie," laughed the Professor.

"And it's that way about lots of things," said Louie a little plaintively.

"Kitty," said Scott as they were driving home that night, Kathleen in the driver's seat beside him, "that silver bracelet Louie spoke of was one of Tom's trinkets, wasn't it? Do you suppose she has some feeling for him still, under all this pomposity?"

"I don't know, and I don't care. But, oh, Scott, I do love you very much!" she cried vehemently.

He pinched off his driving-glove between his knees and snuggled his hand over hers, inside her muff. "Sure?" he muttered.

"Yes, I *do!*" she said fiercely, squeezing his knuckles together with all her might.

"Awful nice of you to have told me all about it at

the start, Kitty. Most girls wouldn't have thought it necessary. I'm the only one who knows, ain't I?"

"The only one who ever has known."

"And I'm just the one another girl wouldn't have told. Why did you, Kit?"

"I don't know. I suppose even then I must have had a feeling that you were the real one." Her head dropped on his shoulder. "You know you *are* the real one, don't you?"

"I guess!"

TEN

That winter there was a meeting of an Association of Electrical Engineers in Hamilton. Louie Marsellus, who was a member, gave a luncheon for the visiting engineers at the Country Club, and then motored them to Outland. Scott McGregor was at the lunch, with the other newspaper men. On his return he stopped at the university and picked up his father-in-law.

"I'll run you over home. Which house, the old? How did you get out of Louie's party?"

"I had classes."

"It was some lunch! Louie's a good host. First-rate cigars, and plenty of them," Scott tapped his breast-pocket. "We had poor Tom served up again. It was all right, of course—the scientific men were interested, didn't know much about him. Louie called on me for personal recollections; he was very polite about it. I didn't express myself very well. I'm not much of a speaker, anyhow, and this time I seemed to be talking uphill. You know, Tom isn't very real to me any more. Sometimes I think he was just a—a glittering idea. Here we are, Doctor."

Scott's remark rather troubled the Professor. He went up the two flights of stairs and sat down in his shadowy crypt at the top of the house. With his right elbow on the table, his eyes on the floor, he began recalling as clearly and definitely as he could every incident of that bright, windy spring day when he first saw Tom Outland.

He was working in his garden one Saturday morning, when a young man in a heavy winter suit and a Stetson hat, carrying a grey canvas telescope, came in at the green door that led from the street.

"Are you Professor St. Peter?" he inquired.

Upon being assured, he set down his bag on the gravel, took out a blue cotton handkerchief, and wiped his face, which was covered with beads of moisture. The first thing the Professor noticed about the visitor was his manly, mature voice—low, calm, experienced, very different from the thin ring or the hoarse shouts of boyish voices about the campus. The next thing he observed was the strong line of contrast below the young man's sandy hair—the very fair forehead which had been protected by his hat, and the reddish brown of his face, which had evidently been exposed to a stronger sun than the spring sun of Hamilton. The boy was fine-looking, he saw—tall and presumably well built, though the shoulders of his stiff, heavy coat were so preposterously padded that the upper part of him seemed shut up in a case.

"I want to go to school here, Professor St. Peter, and I've come to ask your advice. I don't know anybody in the town."

"You want to enter the university, I take it? What high school are you from?"

"I've never been to high school, sir. That's the trouble."

"Why, yes. I hardly see how you can enter the university. Where are you from?"

"New Mexico. I haven't been to school, but I've studied. I read Latin with a priest down there."

St. Peter smiled incredulously. "How much Latin?"

"I read Cæsar and Virgil, the *Æneid.*"

"How many books?"

"We went right through." He met the Professor's questions squarely, his eyes were resolute, like his voice.

"Oh, you did." St. Peter stood his spade against the wall. He had been digging around his red-fruited thorn-trees. "Can you repeat any of it?"

The boy began: *"Infandum, regina, jubes renovare dolorem,"* and steadily continued for fifty lines or more, until St. Peter held up a checking hand.

"Excellent. Your priest was a thorough Latinist. You have a good pronunciation and good intonation. Was the Father by any chance a Frenchman?"

"Yes, sir. He was a missionary priest, from Belgium."

"Did you learn any French from him?"

"No, sir. He wanted to practise his Spanish."

"You speak Spanish?"

"Not very well, Mexican Spanish."

The Professor tried him out in Spanish and told him he thought he knew enough to get credit for a modern language. "And what are your deficiencies?"

"I've never had any mathematics or science, and I write a very bad hand."

"That's not unusual," St. Peter told him. "But, by the way, how did you happen to come to me instead of to the registrar?"

"I just got in this morning, and your name was the only one here I knew. I read an article by you in a magazine, about Fray Marcos. Father Duchene said it was the only thing with any truth in it he'd read about our country down there."

The Professor had noticed before that whenever he wrote for popular periodicals it got him into trouble. "Well, what are your plans, young man? And, by the way, what is your name?"

"Tom Outland."

The Professor repeated it. It seemed to suit the boy exactly.

"How old are you?"

"I'm twenty." He blushed, and St. Peter supposed he was dropping off a few years, but he found afterward that the boy didn't know exactly how old he was. "I thought I might get a tutor and make up my mathematics this summer."

"Yes, that could be managed. How are you fixed for money?"

Outland's face grew grave. "I'm rather awkwardly fixed. If you were to write to Tarpin, New Mexico, to inquire about me, you'd find I have money in the bank there, and you'd think I had been deceiving you. But it's money I can't touch while I'm able-bodied. It's in trust for someone else. But I've got three hundred dollars without any string on it, and I'm hoping to get work here. I've been bossing a section gang all winter, and I'm in good condition. I'll do anything but wait table. I won't do that." On this point he seemed to feel strongly.

The Professor learned some of his story that morning. His parents, he said, were "mover people," and both died when they were crossing southern Kansas in a prairie schooner. He was a baby and had been informally adopted by some kind people who took care of his mother in her last hours,—a locomotive engineer named O'Brien, and his wife. This engineer was transferred to New Mexico and took the foundling boy along with his own children. As soon as Tom was old enough to work, he got a job as call boy and did his share toward supporting the family.

"What's a call boy, a messenger boy?"

"No, sir. It's a more responsible position. Our town was an important freight division on the Santa Fé, and a lot of train men live there. The freight schedule is always changing, because it's a single track road and the dispatcher has to get the freights through when he can. Suppose you're a brakeman, and your train is due out at two A.M.; well, like as not, it will be changed to midnight, or to four in the morning. You go to bed as if you were going to sleep all night, with nothing on your mind. The call boy watches the schedule board, and half an hour before your train goes out, he comes and taps on your window and gets you up in time to make it. The call boy has to be on to things in the town. He must know when there's a poker game on, and how to slip in easy. You can't tell when there's a spotter about, and if a man's reported for gambling, he's fired. Sometimes you have to get a man when he isn't where he ought to be. I found there was usually a reason at home for that." The boy spoke with gravity, as if he had reflected deeply upon irregular behaviour.

Just then Mrs. St. Peter came out into the garden and asked her husband if he wouldn't bring his young friend in to lunch. Outland started and looked with panic toward the door by which he had come in; but the Professor wouldn't hear of his going, and picked up his telescope to prevent his escape. As he carried it into the house and put it down in the hall, he noticed that it was strangely light for its bulk. Mrs. St. Peter introduced the guest to her two little girls, and asked him if he didn't want to go upstairs to wash his hands. He disappeared; as he came back something disconcerting happened. The front hall and the front staircase were the only hard wood in the house, but as Tom came down the waxed steps, his heavy new shoes shot out from under him, and he sat down on the end of his spine with a thump. Little Kathleen burst into a giggle, and her elder sister looked at her reprovingly; Mrs. St. Peter apologized for the stairs.

"I'm not much used to stairs, living mostly in 'dobe houses," Tom explained, as he picked himself up.

At luncheon the boy was very silent at first. He sat looking admiringly at Mrs. St. Peter and the little girls. The day had grown warm, and the Professor thought this was the hottest boy he had ever seen. His stiff white collar began to melt, and his handkerchief, as he kept wiping his face with it, became a rag. "I didn't know it would be so warm up here, or I'd have picked a lighter suit," he said, embarrassed by the activity of his skin.

"We would like to hear more about your life in the South-west," said his host. "How long were you a call boy?"

"Two years. Then I had pneumonia, and the doctor said I ought to go on the range, so I went to work for a big cattle firm."

Mrs. St. Peter began to question him about the Indian pueblos. He was reticent at first, but he presently warmed up in defence of Indian house-wifery. He forgot his shyness so far, indeed, that having made a neat heap of mashed potato beside his chop, he conveyed it to his mouth on the blade of his knife, at which sight the little girls were not able to conceal their astonishment. Mrs. St. Peter went on quietly talking about Indian pottery and asking him where they made the best.

"I think the very best is the old,—the cliff-dweller pottery," he said. "Do you take an interest in pottery,

Ma'am? Maybe you'd like to see some I have brought along." As they rose from the table he went to his telescope underneath the hat-rack, knelt beside it, and undid the straps. When he lifted the cover, it seemed full of bulky objects wrapped in newspapers. After feeling among them, he unwrapped one and displayed an earthen water jar, shaped like those common in Greek sculpture, and ornamented with a geometrical pattern in black and white.

"That's one of the real old ones. I know, for I got it out myself. I don't know just how old, but there's piñon trees three hundred years old by their rings, growing up in the stone trail that leads to the ruins where I got it."

"Stone trail . . . piñons?" she asked.

"Yes, deep, narrow trails in white rock, worn by their moccasin feet coming and going for generations. And these old piñon trees have come up in the trails since the race died off. You can tell something about how long ago it was by them." He showed her a coating of black on the under side of the jar.

"That's not from the firing. See, I can scratch it off. It's soot, from when it was on the cook-fire last—and that was before Columbus landed, I guess. Nothing makes those people seem so real to me as their old pots, with the fire-black on them." As she gave it back to him, he shook his head. "That one's for you, Ma'am, if you like it."

"Oh, I couldn't think of letting you give it to me! You must keep it for yourself, or put it in a museum." But that seemed to touch a sore spot.

"Museums," he said bitterly, "they don't care about our things. They want something that came from Crete or Egypt. I'd break my jars sooner than they should get them. But I'd like this one to have a good home, among your nice things"—he looked about appreciatively. "I've no place to keep them. They're in my way, especially that big one. My trunk is at the station, but I was afraid to leave the pottery. You don't get them out whole like that very often."

"But get them out of what, from where? I want to know all about it."

"Maybe some day, Ma'am, I can tell you," he said, wiping his sooty fingers on his handkerchief. His reply was courteous but final. He strapped his bag and picked up his hat, then hesitated and smiled. Taking a buck-skin bag from his pocket, he walked over to the window-seat where the children were, and held out his hand to them, saying: "These I would like to give to the little girls." In his palm lay two lumps of soft blue stone, the colour of robins' eggs, or of the sea on halcyon days of summer.

The children marvelled. "Oh, what are they?"

"Turquoises, just the way they come out of the mine, before the jewellers have tampered with them and made them look green. The Indians like them this way."

Again Mrs. St. Peter demurred. She told him very

kindly that she couldn't let him give his stones to the children. "They are worth a lot of money."

"I'd never sell them. They were given to me by a friend. I have a lot, and they're no use to me, but they'll make pretty playthings for little girls." His voice was so wistful and winning that there was nothing to do.

"Hold them still a moment," said the Professor, looking down, not at the turquoises, but at the hand that held them: the muscular, many-lined palm, the long, strong fingers with soft ends, the straight little finger, the flexible, beautifully shaped thumb that curved back from the rest of the hand as if it were its own master. What a hand! He could see it yet, with the blue stones lying in it.

In a moment the stranger was gone, and the St. Peter family sat down and looked at one another. He remembered just what his wife had said on that occasion.

"Well, this is something new in students, Godfrey. We ask a poor perspiring tramp boy to lunch, to save his pennies, and he departs leaving princely gifts."

Yes, the Professor reflected, after all these years, that was still true. Fellows like Outland don't carry much luggage, yet one of the things you know them by is their sumptuous generosity—and when they are gone, all you can say of them is that they departed leaving princely gifts.

With a good tutor, young Outland had no difficulty

in making up three years' mathematics in four months. Latin, he owned, had been hard for him. But in mathematics, he didn't have to work, he had merely to give his attention. His tutor had never known anything like it. But St. Peter held the boy at arm's length. As a young teacher full of zeal, he had been fooled more than once. He knew that the wonderful seldom holds water, that brilliancy has no staying power, and the unusual becomes commonplace by a natural law.

In those first months Mrs. St. Peter saw more of their protégé than her husband did. She found him a good boarding-place, took care that he had proper summer clothes and that he no longer addressed her as "Ma'am." He came often to the house that summer, to play with the little girls. He would spend hours with them in the garden, making Hopi villages with sand and pebbles, drawing maps of the Painted Desert and the Rio Grande country in the gravel, telling them stories, when there was no one by to listen, about the adventures he had had with his friend Roddy.

"Mother," Kathleen broke out one evening at dinner, "what do you think! Tom hasn't any birthday."

"How is that?"

"When his mother died in the mover wagon, and Tom was a baby, she forgot to tell the O'Briens when his birthday was. She even forgot to tell them how old he was. They thought he must be a year and a half, because he was so big, but Mrs. O'Brien always said he didn't have enough teeth for that."

St. Peter asked her whether Tom had ever said how it happened that his mother died in a wagon.

"Well, you see, she was very sick, and they were going West for her health. And one day, when they were camped beside a river, Tom's father went in to swim, and had a cramp or something, and was drowned. Tom's mother saw it, and it made her worse. She was there all alone, till some people found her and drove her on to the next town to a doctor. But when they got her there, she was too sick to leave the wagon. They drove her into the O'Briens' yard, because that was nearest the doctor's and Mrs. O'Brien was a kind woman. And she died in a few hours."

"Does Tom know anything about his father?"

"Nothing except that he was a school-teacher in Missouri. His mother told the O'Briens that much. But the O'Briens were just lovely to him."

St. Peter had noticed that in the stories Tom told the children there were no shadows. Kathleen and Rosamond regarded his free-lance childhood as a gay adventure they would gladly have shared. They loved to play at being Tom and Roddy. Roddy was the remarkable friend, ten years older than Tom, who knew everything about snakes and panthers and deserts and Indians. "And he gave up a fine job firing on the Santa Fé, and went off with Tom to ride after cattle for hardly any wages, just to be with Tom and take care of him after he'd had pneumonia," Kathleen told them.

"That wasn't the only reason," Rosamond added

dreamily. "Roddy was proud. He didn't like taking orders and living on pay cheques. He liked to be free, and to sit in his saddle all day and use it for a pillow at night. You know Tom said that, Kitty."

"Anyhow, he was noble. He was always noble, noble Roddy!" Kathleen finished it off.

After the first day, when he had walked into the garden and introduced himself, Tom never took up the story of his own life again, either with the Professor or Mrs. St. Peter, though he was often encouraged to do so. He would talk about the New Mexico country when questioned, about Father Duchene, the missionary priest who had been his teacher, about the Indians; but only with the two little girls did he ever speak freely and confidentially about himself. St. Peter used to wonder how the boy could afford to spend so much time with the children. All through that summer and fall he used to come in the afternoon and join them in the garden. In the winter he dropped in two or three evenings a week to play Five Hundred or to take a dancing-lesson.

There was evidently something enchanting about the atmosphere of the house to a boy who had always lived a rough life. He enjoyed the prettiness and freshness and gaiety of the little girls as if they were flowers. Probably, too, he liked being so attractive to them. A flush of pleasure would come over Tom's face—so much fairer now than when he first arrived in Hamilton—if Kathleen caught his hand and tried to squeeze it hard enough to hurt, crying: "Oh, Tom, *tell* us about the time you and Roddy found the water hole dry, and then afterward tell us about when the rattlesnake bit Henry!" He would whisper: "Pretty soon," and after a while, through the open windows, the Professor would hear them in the garden: the laughter and exclamations of the little girls, and that singularly individual voice of Tom's—mature, confident, seldom varying in pitch, but full of slight, very moving modulations.

He couldn't have wished for a better companion for his daughters, and they were teaching Tom things that he needed more than mathematics.

Sitting thus in his study, long afterward, St. Peter reflected that those first years, before Outland had done anything remarkable, were really the best of all. He liked to remember the charming groups of three he was always coming upon,—in the hammock swung between the linden-trees, in the window-seat, or before the dining-room fire. Oh, there had been fine times in this old house then: family festivals and hospitalities, little girls dancing in and out, Augusta coming and going, gay dresses hanging in his study at night, Christmas shopping and secrets and smothered laughter on the stairs. When a man had lovely children in his house, fragrant and happy, full of pretty fancies and generous impulses, why couldn't he keep them? Was there no way but Medea's, he wondered?

ELEVEN

St. Peter had come in late from an afternoon lecture, and had just lighted his kerosene lamp to go to work, when he heard a light foot ascending the stairs. In a moment Kathleen's voice called: "May I interrupt for a moment, Papa?"

He opened the door and drew her in.

"Kitty, do you remember the time you sat out there with your bee-sting and your bottle? Nobody ever showed me more consideration than that, not even your mother."

Kathleen threw her hat and jacket into the sewing-chair and walked about, touching things to see how dusty they were. "I've been wondering if you didn't need me to come in and clean house for you, but it's not so bad as they report it. This is the first time I've called on you since you've been here alone. I've turned in from the walk more than once, but I've always run away again." She paused to warm her hands at the little stove. "I'm silly, you know; such queer things make me blue. And you still have Augusta's old forms. I don't think anything ever happened to her that amused her so much. And now, you know, she's quite sentimental about their being here. It's about Augusta that I came, Papa. Did you know that she had lost some of her savings in the Kinkoo Copper Company?"

"Augusta? Are you sure? What a shame!"

"Yes. She was sewing for me last week. I noticed that she seemed depressed and hadn't much appetite for lunch—which, you know, is unusual for Augusta. She was ashamed to tell any of us about it, because it seems she'd asked Louie's advice, and he told her not to invest in that company. But a lot of people in her church were putting money into it, and of course that made it seem all right to her. She lost five hundred dollars, a fortune for her, and Scott says she'll never get a cent of it back."

"Five hundred dollars," murmured St. Peter. "Let me see, at three dollars a day that means one hundred and sixty-six days. Now what can we do about it?"

"Of course we must do something. I knew you'd feel that way, Father."

"Certainly. Among us, we must cover it. I'll speak to Rosamond to-night."

"You needn't, dear." Kathleen tossed her head. "I have been to her. She refuses."

"Refuses? She can't refuse, my dear. I'll have a word to say." The firmness of his tone, and the quick rush of claret colour under his skin, were a gratification to his daughter.

"She says that Louie took the trouble to speak to his banker and to several copper men before he advised Augusta; and that if she doesn't learn her lesson this time, she will do the same thing over again. Rosamond said they would do something for Augusta later, but she didn't say what."

"Leave Rosamond to me. I'll convince her."

"Even if you can do anything with her, she's determined to make Augusta admit her folly, and it can't be done that way. Augusta is terribly proud. When I told her her customers ought to make it up to her, she was very haughty and said she wasn't that kind of a sewing-woman; that she gave her ladies good measure for their money. Scott thought we could buy stock in some good company and tell her we had used our influence and got an exchange, but that she must keep quiet about it. We could manage some such little fib, she knows so little about business. I know I can get the Dudleys and the Browns to help. We needn't go to the Marselluses."

"Wait a few days. It's a disgrace to us as a family not to make it up ourselves. On her own account, we oughtn't to let Rosamond out. She's altogether too blind to responsibilities of that kind. In a world full of blunderers, why should Augusta have to pay scrupulously for her mistakes? It's very petty of Rosie, really!"

Kathleen started to speak, stopped and turned away. "Scott will give a hundred dollars," she said a moment later.

"That's very generous of him. I'll give another, and Rosie shall make up the rest. If she doesn't, I'll speak to Louie. He's an absolutely generous chap. I've never known him to refuse to give either time or money."

Kathleen's eyes suddenly brightened. "Why, Daddy, you have Tom's Mexican blanket! I never knew he gave it to you. I've often wondered what became of it." She picked up from the foot of the box-couch a purple blanket, faded in streaks to amethyst, with a pale yellow stripe at either end.

"Oh, yes, I often get chilly when I lie down, especially if I turn the stove out, which your mother says I ought always to do. Nothing could part me from that blanket."

"He wouldn't have given it to anybody but you. It was like his skin. Do you remember how horsey it smelled when he first brought it over and showed it to us?"

"Just like a livery stable! It had been strapped behind the saddle on so many sweating cow-ponies. In damp weather that smell is still perceptible."

Kathleen stroked it thoughtfully. "Roddy brought it up from Old Mexico, you know. He gave it to Tom that winter he had pneumonia. Tom ought to have taken it to France with him. He used to say that Rodney Blake might turn up in the Foreign Legion. If he had taken this, it might have been like the wooden cups that were always revealing *Amis* and *Amile* to each other."

St. Peter smiled and patted her hand on the blanket.

———

"Do you know, Kitty, I sometimes think I ought to go out and look for Blake myself. He's on my conscience. If that country down there weren't so everlastingly big—"

"Oh, Father! That was my romantic dream when I was little, finding Roddy! I used to think about it for hours when I was supposed to be taking my nap. I used to swim rivers and climb mountains and wander about with Navajos, and rescue Roddy at the most critical moments, when he was being stabbed in the back, or drugged in a gambling-house, and bring him back to Tom. You know Tom told us about him long before he ever told you."

"You children used to live in his stories. You cared more about them than about all your adventure books."

"I still do," said Kathleen, rising. "Now that Rosamond has Outland, I consider Tom's mesa entirely my own."

St. Peter put down the cigarette he had just lighted with anticipation. "Can't you stay awhile, Kitty? I almost never see anyone who remembers that side of Tom. It was nice, all those years when he was in and out of the house like an older brother. Always very different from the other college boys, wasn't he? Always had something in his voice, in his eyes . . . One seemed to catch glimpses of an unusual background behind his shoulders when he came into the room."

Kathleen smiled wanly. "Yes, and now he's all turned out chemicals and dollars and cents, hasn't he? But not

for you and me! Our Tom is much nicer than theirs."
She put on her jacket and went out of the study and
quickly down the stairs. Her father, on the landing,
looked after her until she disappeared. When she was
gone he still stood there, motionless, as if he were
listening intently, or trying to fasten upon some fugitive
idea.

TWELVE

St. Peter was breakfasting at six-thirty, alone, reading last night's letters while he waited for the coffee to percolate. It had been long since he had had an eight o'clock class, but this year the schedule committee had slyly put him down for one. "He can afford to take a taxi over now," the Dean remarked.

After breakfast he went upstairs and into his wife's room. "I have a rendezvous with a lady," he said, tossing an envelope upon her counterpane. She read a note from Mrs. Crane, the least attractive of the faculty ladies, requesting an interview with the Professor at his earliest convenience: as she wished to see him quite alone, might she come to his study in the old house, where she understood he still worked?

"Poor Godfrey!" murmured his wife.

"One ought not to joke about it——" St. Peter went into his own room to get a handkerchief and came back, taking up his suspended sentence. "I'm afraid it means poor Crane is coming up for another operation. Or, worse still, that the surgeons tell her another would be useless. It's like *The Pit and the Pendulum*. I feel as if the poor fellow were strapped down on a revolving disk that comes around under the knife just so often."

Mrs. St. Peter looked judicially at the letter, then at her husband's back. She didn't believe that surgery would be the subject of discussion when they met. Mrs. Crane had been behaving very strangely of late.

Doctor Crane had married a girl whom no other man ever thought of courting, a girl of whom people always said: "Oh, she's so *good!*" chiefly because she was so homely. They had three very plain daughters, and only Crane's salary to live upon. Doctors and surgeons kept them poor enough.

St. Peter kissed his wife and went forth quite unconscious of what was going on in her mind. During the morning he telephoned Mrs. Crane, and arranged a meeting with her at five o'clock. As the bell in the old house didn't work now, he waited downstairs on the front porch, to receive his visitor and conduct her up to his study. It was raining drearily, and Mrs. Crane arrived in a rubber coat, and a knitted sport hat belonging to one of her daughters. St. Peter took her wet umbrella and led her up the two flights of stairs.

"I'm not very well appointed to receive ladies, Mrs. Crane. This was the sewing-room, you know. There's Augusta's chair, which she insisted was comfortable."

"Thank you." Mrs. Crane sat down, took off her gloves, and tucked wisps of damp hair up under her crocheted hat. Her bleak, plain face wore an expression of grievance.

"I've come without my husband's knowledge, Doctor St. Peter, to ask you what you think can be done about our rights in the Outland patent. You know how my husband's health has crippled us financially, and we never know when his trouble may come on worse again. Myself, I've never doubted that you would see it is only right to share with us."

St. Peter looked at her in amazement. "But, my dear Mrs. Crane, how can I share with you what I haven't got? Tom willed his estate and royalties in a perfectly regular way. The fact that he named my daughter as his sole beneficiary doesn't affect me, any more than if he had named some relative of his own. I tell you frankly, I have never received one dollar from the Outland patent."

"It's all the same if it goes to your family, Doctor St. Peter. My husband must be considered in this matter. He spent days and nights working with Outland. Tom never could have worked his theory out without Robert's help. He said so, more than once, in my presence and in the presence of others."

"Oh, I believe that, Mrs. Crane. But the difficulty is that Tom didn't make any recognition of that assistance in his will."

Mrs. Crane had set her head and advanced her long chin with meek determination. "Well, this is how it was, Professor. Mr. Marsellus came here a stranger, to put in the Edison power plant, just at the time the city was stirred up about Outland's being killed at the front. Everybody was wanting to do something in recognition of the young man. You brought Mr. Marsellus to our house and introduced him. After that he came alone, again and again, and he got round my husband. Robert thought he was disinterested, and was only taking a scientific interest, and he told him a great deal about what he and Outland had been working on. Then Rosamond's lawyers came for the papers. Tom Outland had no laboratory of his own. He was allowed the use of a room in the physics building, at my husband's request. He wanted to be there, because he constantly needed Robert's help. The first thing we knew, your daughter's engagement to Marsellus was announced, and then we heard that all Outland's papers had been given over to him."

Here St. Peter anticipated her. "But, Mrs. Crane, your husband couldn't, and wouldn't, have kept Tom's papers. They had to be given over to his executor, who was my daughter's attorney."

"Well, I could have kept them, if he couldn't!"—Mrs. Crane threw up her head as if to show that the worm had turned at last—"kept them until justice was done us, and some recognition had been made of my husband's part in all that research work. If he had taken the papers to court then, with all the evidence we have, we could easily have got an equity. But Mr. Marsellus is very smooth. He flattered Robert and got everything there was."

"But he didn't get anything from your husband. Outland's papers and apparatus were delivered to his executor, as was inevitable."

"That was a poor subterfuge," said Mrs. Crane, with

deep meaning. "You know how unworldly Robert is, and as an old friend you might have warned us."

"Of what, Mrs. Crane?"

"Why, that Marsellus saw there was a fortune in the gas my husband and his pupil had made, and we could have asked for our equity before we gave your son-in-law a free hand with everything."

St. Peter felt very unhappy. He began walking up and down the little room. "Heaven knows I'd like to see Crane get something out of it, but how? How? I've thought a great deal about this matter, and I've blamed Tom for making that kind of will. I don't think it occurred to the boy that the will would ever be probated. He expected to come back from the war and develop the thing himself. I doubt whether Robert, with all his superior knowledge, would have known the twists and turns by which the patent could be commercialized. It took a great deal of work and a special kind of ability to do that."

"A salesman's ability!" Mrs. Crane was becoming nasty.

"If you like; but certainly Robert would have been no man to convince manufacturers and machinists, any more than I would. A great deal of money was put into it, too, before any came back; every cent Marsellus had, and all he could borrow. He took heavy chances. Crane and I together could never have raised a hundredth part of the capital that was necessary to get the thing started. Without capital to make it go, Tom's idea was merely a formula written out on paper. It had lain for two years in your husband's laboratory, and would have lain there for years more before he or I would have done anything about it."

Mrs. Crane's dreary face took on more animation than he had supposed it capable of. "It had lain there because it belonged there, and was made there! My husband was done out of it by an adventurer, and his friendship for you tied his hands. I must say you've shown very little consideration for him. You might have warned us never to let those papers go. You see Robert getting weaker all the time and having those terrible operations, and our girls going shabby and teaching in the ward schools, and Rosamond riding about in a limousine and building country houses,—and you do nothing about it. You take your honours—you've deserved them, we never forget that—and move into your new house, and you don't remember what it is to be in straitened circumstances."

St. Peter drew his chair nearer to Mrs. Crane, and addressed her patiently. "Mrs. Crane, if you had any legal rights in the patent, I'd defend them against Rosamond as soon as against anyone else. I think she ought to recognize Dr. Crane's long friendship and helpfulness to Tom in some way. I don't see just how it can be done, but I feel it should be. And if you wish, I'll tell Rosamond how I feel. Why don't you put this matter before her?"

"I don't care to ask anything of Mrs. Marsellus. I

wrote her some time ago, and she replied to me through her lawyer, saying that all claims against the Outland patent would be considered in due order. It's not worthy of a man in Robert's position to accept hush money from the Marselluses. We want justice, and my brother is confident the court will give it to us."

"Well, I suppose Bright knows more about what the courts will do than I. But if you've decided to go to law about it, why did you come to me?"

"There are some things the law don't cover," said Mrs. Crane mysteriously, as she rose and put on her gloves. "I wanted you to know how we feel about it."

St. Peter followed her downstairs and put up her umbrella for her, and then went back to his study to think it over. His friendship with Crane had been a strange one. Out in the world they would almost certainly have kept clear of each other; but in the university they had fought together in a common cause. Both, with all their might, had resisted the new commercialism, the aim to "show results" that was undermining and vulgarizing education. The State Legislature and the board of regents seemed determined to make a trade school of the university. Candidates for the degree of Bachelor of Arts were allowed credits for commercial studies; courses in book-keeping, experimental farming, domestic science, dress-making, and what not. Every year the regents tried to diminish the number of credits required in science and the humanities. The liberal appropriations, the promotions and increases in salary, all went to the professors who worked with the regents to abolish the purely cultural studies. Out of a faculty of sixty, there were perhaps twenty men who made any serious stand for scholarship, and Robert Crane was one of the staunchest. He had lost the Deanship of the College of Science because of his uncompromising opposition to the degrading influence of politicians in university affairs. The honour went, instead, to a much younger man, head of the department of chemistry, who was willing "to give the taxpayers what they wanted."

The struggle to preserve the dignity of the university, and their own, had brought St. Peter and Dr. Crane much together. They were, moreover, the only two men on the faculty who were doing research work of an uncommercial nature, and they occasionally dropped in on one another to exchange ideas. But that was as far as it went. St. Peter couldn't ask Crane to dinner; the presence of a bottle of claret on the table would have made him uncomfortable. Dr. Crane had all the prejudices of the Baptist community in which he grew up. He carried them with him when he went to study at a German university, and brought them back. But Crane knew that none of his colleagues followed his work so closely, and rejoiced at his little triumphs so heartily, as St. Peter.

St. Peter couldn't help admiring the man's courage; poor, ill, overworked, held by his conscience to a generous discharge of his duties as a teacher, he was all the while carrying on these tedious and delicate experiments that had to do with determining the extent of space. Fortunately, Crane seemed to have no social needs or impulses. He never went anywhere, except, once or twice a year, to a dinner at the President's house. Music disturbed him too much, dancing shocked him—he couldn't see why it was permitted among the students. Once, after Mrs. St. Peter had sat next him at the President's dinner-table, she said to her husband: "The man is too dreary! All evening his heavy underwear kept coming down below his cuffs, and he kept poking it back with his fore-finger. I believe he thinks it's wicked to live with even so plain a woman as Mrs. Crane."

After Tom Outland graduated from the university, he and Dr. Crane worked side by side in the Physics building for several years. The older man had been of great assistance to the younger, without doubt. Though that kind of help, the result of criticism and suggestion, is not easily reckoned in percentages, still St. Peter thought Crane ought to get something out of the patent. He resolved to see Louie about it. But first he had better talk with Crane himself, and try to dissuade him from going to law. His brother-in-law, Homer Bright, would be tempted by the publicity which an action involving the Outland patent would certainly bring him. But he would lose the case, and Crane would get nothing. Whereas Louie, if he were properly approached, would be generous.

St. Peter looked at his watch. He would go home now, and after dinner he would walk over to the Physics building, where his colleague worked every night. He never went to see Crane at his house if he could help it. He lived in the most depressing and unnecessary ugliness.

At dinner Lillian asked him no questions about his interview with Mrs. Crane, and he volunteered no information. She was not surprised, however, when he said he would not stop for a cigar, as he was going over to the Physics laboratory.

He walked through the park, past the old house and across the north end of the campus, to a building that stood off by itself in a grove of pine-trees. It was constructed of red brick, after an English model. The architect had had a good idea, and he very nearly succeeded in making a good thing, something like the old Smithsonian building in Washington. But after it was begun, the State Legislature had defeated him by grinding down the contractor to cheap execution, and had spoiled everything, outside and in. Ever since it was finished, plumbers and masons and carpenters had been kept busy patching and repairing it. Crane and St. Peter, both young men then, had wasted weeks of time with the contractors, and had finally gone before the Legislative committee in person to plead for the integrity of that building. But nothing came of all their pains. It was one of many lost causes.

St. Peter entered the building and went upstairs to a small room at the end of a chain of laboratories. After knocking, he heard the familiar shuffle of Crane's carpet slippers, and the door opened.

Crane was wearing a grey cotton coat, shrunk to a rag by washing, though he wasn't working with fluids or batteries to-night, but at a roll-top desk littered with papers. The room was like any study behind a lecture room; dusty books, dusty files, but no apparatus—except a spirit-lamp and a little saucepan in which the physicist heated water for his cocoa at regular intervals. He was working by the glare of an unshaded electric bulb of high power—the man seemed to have no feeling for comfort of any kind. He asked his visitor to sit down, and to excuse him for a moment while he copied some entries into a note-book.

St. Peter watched him scribbling with his fountain pen. The hands that were so deft in delicate manipulations were white and soft-looking; the fingers long and loosely hung, stained with chemicals, and blunted at the tips like a violinist's. His head was square, and the lower part of his face was covered by a reddish, matted beard. His pale eyes and fawn-coloured eyebrows were outbalanced by his mouth, his most conspicuous feature. One always remembered about Crane that unexpected, startling red mouth in a setting of kinky beard. The lips had no modelling, they were as thick at the corners as in the middle, and he spoke through them rather than with them. He seemed painfully conscious of them.

St. Peter saw no use in beating about the bush. As soon as Crane put down his pen, he remarked that Mrs. Crane had been to see him that afternoon. His colleague flushed, took up a large celluloid paper-knife, and began shutting and unshutting his hands about the blade.

"I want to know exactly how you feel about this, and what the facts are," St. Peter began. "We've never discussed it before, and there may be things I know nothing about. Did Tom ever say that he meant you to have a share in his profits, if there were any?"

"No, not exactly. Not exactly that." Dr. Crane moved his shoulders about in his tight coat and looked embarrassed and unhappy. "More than once he said, in a general way, that he hoped it would go, on my account as well as on his own, and that we would use the income for further experiments."

"Did he talk much about the possible commercial value of the gas while he was trying to make it?"

"Not much. No, very seldom. Perhaps not more than half a dozen times in the three years he was working in my laboratory. But whenever he did, he spoke as if there would be something in it for both of us if our gas became remunerative."

"Just how much was it 'our gas,' Crane?"

"Strictly speaking, of course, it wasn't. The idea was Outland's. He benefited by my criticism, and I often helped him with his experiments. He never acquired a nice laboratory technic. He would fail repeatedly in some perfectly sound experiment because of careless procedure."

"Do you think he would have arrived at his results without your help?"

Dr. Crane was clenching the paper-knife with both hands. "That I cannot say. He was impatient. He might have got discouraged and turned to something else. He would have been much slower in getting his results, at any rate. His conception was right, but very delicate manipulation was necessary, and he was a careless experimentor."

St. Peter felt that this was becoming nothing less than cross-examination. He tried to change the tone of it.

"I want to see you get recognition and compensation for whatever part you had in his experiments, if there's any way to get it. But you've been neglectful, Crane. You haven't taken the proper steps. Why in the world didn't you have some understanding with Tom when he was getting his patent? You knew all about it."

"It didn't occur to me then. We'd finished the experiments, and I put them out of my mind. I was trying to concentrate on my own work. His results weren't as interesting scientifically as I'd expected them to be."

"While his manuscripts and formulæ were lying here those two years, did you ever make the gas, or give any study to its behaviour?"

"No, of course not. It's off my own line, and didn't interest me."

"Then it's only since this patent has begun to make money that it does interest you?"

Dr. Crane twisted his shoulders. "Yes. It's the money."

"Heaven knows I'd like to see you get some of it. But why did you put it off so long? Why didn't you make some claim when you delivered the papers to his executor, since you hadn't done so before? Why didn't you bring the matter up to me then, and let me make a claim against the estate for you?"

Dr. Crane could endure his chair no longer. He began to walk softly about in his slippers, looking at nothing, but, as he talked, picking up objects here and there,—drawing-tools, his cocoa-cup, a china cream-pitcher, turning them round and carefully putting them down again, just as he often absently handled pieces of apparatus when he was lecturing.

"I know," he said, "appearances are against me. But you must understand my negligence. You know how little opportunity a man has to carry on his own line of investigation here. You know how much time I give to any of my students who are doing honest work. Outland was, of course, the most brilliant pupil I ever had, and I gave him time and thought without stint. Gladly, of course. If he were reaping the rewards of his discovery himself, I'd have nothing to say—though I've not the least doubt he would compensate me liberally. But it does not seem right that a stranger should profit, and not those who helped him. You, of course, do profit—indirectly, if not directly. You cannot shut your eyes to the fact that this money, coming into your family, has strengthened your credit and your general security. That's as it should be. But your claim was less definite than mine. I spent time and strength I could ill afford to spare on the very series of experiments that led to this result. Marsellus gets the benefit of my work as well as of Outland's. I have certainly been ill-used—and, as you say, it's difficult to get recompense when I ask for it so late. It's not to my discredit, certainly, that I didn't take measures to protect my interests. I never thought of my student's work in terms of money. There were others who did, and I was not considered," he concluded bitterly.

"Why don't you put in a claim to Marsellus, for your time and expert advice? I think he'd honour it. He is going to live here. He probably doesn't wish to be more unpopular than a suddenly prosperous man is bound to be, and you have many friends. I believe I can convince him that it would be poor policy to disregard any reasonable demand."

"I had thought of that. But my wife's brother advises a different course."

"Ah, yes. Mrs. Crane said something of that sort. Well, Crane, if you're going to law about it, I hope you'll consult a sound lawyer, and you know as well as I that Homer Bright is not one."

Dr. Crane coloured and bridled. "I'm sure you are disinterested, St. Peter, but, frankly, I think your judgment has been warped by events. You don't realize how clear the matter is to unprejudiced minds. Though I'm such an unpractical man, I have evidence to rest my claims upon."

"The more the better, if you are going to depend on such a windbag as Bright. If you go to law, I'd like to see you win your case."

St. Peter said good-night, went down the stairs, and out through the dark pine-trees. Evidence, Crane said; probably letters Tom had written him during the winter he was working at Johns Hopkins. Well, there was nothing to be done, unless he could get old Dr. Hutchins to persuade Crane to employ an intelligent lawyer. Homer Bright's rhetoric might influence a jury in a rape or bigamy case, but it would antagonize a judge in an equity court.

The Professor took a turn in the park before going home. The interview had depressed him, and he was afraid he might be wakeful. He had never seen his colleague in such an unbecoming light before. Crane was narrow, but he was straight; a man you could count on in the shifty game of college politics. He had never been out to get anything for himself. St. Peter would have said that nothing about the vulgar success of Outland's idea could possibly matter to Crane, beyond gratifying his pride as a teacher and friend.

The park was deserted. The arc-lights were turned off. The leafless trees stood quite motionless in the light of the clear stars. The world was sad to St. Peter as he looked about him; the lake-shore country flat and heavy, Hamilton small and tight and airless. The university, his new house, his old house, everything around him, seemed insupportable, as the boat on which he is imprisoned seems to a sea-sick man. Yes, it was possible that the little world, on its voyage among all the stars, might become like that; a boat on which one could travel no longer, from which one could no longer look up and confront those bright rings or revolution.

He brought himself back with a jerk. Ah, yes, Crane; that was the trouble. If Outland were here to-night, he might say with Mark Antony, *My fortunes have corrupted honest men.*

FOURTEEN

At the end of the semester, St. Peter went to Chicago with Rosamond to help her buy things for her country house. He had very much wanted to stay at home and rest—the university work seemed to take it out of him that winter more than ever before; but Rosamond had set her mind on his going, and Mrs. St. Peter told him he couldn't refuse. A Chicago merchant had brought over a lot of old Spanish furniture, and on this no-body's judgment would be better than St. Peter's. He was supposed to know a good deal about rugs, too. When his wife said a thing must be done, the Professor usually did it, from long-established habit. Her instincts about what one owed to other people were better than his.

Louie accompanied them to Chicago, where he was to join his brother, the one who was in the silk trade in China, and go on to New York with him for a family reunion. St. Peter was amused, and pleased, to see that Louie sincerely hated to leave them—with very little encouragement he would have sent his brother on alone and remained in Chicago with his wife and father-in-law. They all lunched together, after which the Professor and Rosamond took the Marsellus brothers to the LaSalle Street station. When Louie had again and again kissed his hand to them from the rear platform of the Twentieth Century observation car, and was rolled away in the very act of shouting something to his wife, St. Peter, who had so often complained that there was too much Louie in his life, now felt a sudden drop, a distinct sense of loss.

He took Rosamond's arm, and they turned away from the shining rails. "We must be diligent, Rosie. He expects wonders of us."

Scott McGregor got on the Blue Bird Express one afternoon, returning from a business trip for his paper. On entering the smoking-car, he came upon his father-in-law lying back in a leather chair, his clothes covered with dust, his eyes closed, a dead cigar hanging between the relaxed fingers of his dark, muscular hand. It gave Scott a start; he thought the Professor didn't look well.

"Hello, Doctor! What are you doing here? Oh, yes! the shopping expedition. Where's Rosamond?"

"In Chicago. At the Blackstone."

"Outlasted you, did she?"

"That's it." The Professor smiled apologetically, as if he were ashamed to admit it.

Scott sat down beside him and tried to interest him in one subject after another, without success. It occurred to him that he had never before seen the Professor when he seemed absolutely flattened out and listless. That was a bad sign; he was glad they were only half an hour from Hamilton. "The old chap needs rest," he reflected. "Rosamond's run him to death in

Chicago. He oughtn't to be used as a courier, anyhow! I'm going to tell Kitty that we must look out for her father a little. The Marselluses have no mercy, and Lillian has always taken it for granted that he was as strong as three men."

That evening Mrs. St. Peter was standing by the French windows in the drawing-room, watching somewhat anxiously for her husband. The Chicago train was usually punctual, and surely he would have taken a cab from the station, for it was a raw February night with a freezing wind blowing off the lake. St. Peter arrived on foot, however. As he came through the gate, she could see by his walk and the set of his shoulders that he was very tired. She hurried to open the front door, and asked him why he hadn't come up in a taxi.

"Didn't think of it, really. I'm a creature of habit, and that's one of the things I never used to do."

"And in your lightest overcoat! I thought you only wore this one because you were going to buy a new fur coat in Chicago."

"Well, I didn't," he said rather shortly. "Let's omit the verb 'to buy' in all forms for a time. Keep dinner back a little, will you, Lillian? I want to take a warm bath and dress. I did get rather chilled coming up."

Mrs. St. Peter went to the kitchen, and, after a discreet interval, followed her husband upstairs and into his room.

"I know you're tired, but tell me one thing: did you find the painted Spanish bedroom set?"

"Oh, dear, yes! Several of them."

"And were they pretty?"

"Very. At least, I think I'd have found them so if I'd come upon them without so many other things. Too much is certainly worse than too little—of anything. It turned out to be rather an orgy of acquisition."

"Rosamond lost her head?"

"Oh, no! Perfectly cool. I should say she had a faultless purchasing manner. Wonder where a girl who grew up in that old house of ours ever got it. She was like Napoleon looting the Italian palaces."

"Don't be harsh. You had a nice little vacation, at any rate."

"A very expensive one, for a poor professor. And not much rest."

A look of sharp anxiety came into Mrs. St. Peter's face. "You mean," she breathed in a hushed voice, "that she let you——"

He cut in sharply. "I mean that I paid my way, as I hope always to be able to do. Any suggestion to the contrary might have been very graceful, but it would have been rejected. I am quite ready to permit myself a little extravagance to be of service to the women of my family. Any other arrangement is humiliating."

"Then that was why you didn't get your fur coat."

"That may have been one reason. I was not much in the humour for it."

Mrs. St. Peter went swiftly downstairs to make him a cocktail. She sensed an unusual weariness in him, and felt, as it were, the bitter taste on his tongue. A man, she knew, could get from his daughter a peculiar kind of hurt—one of the cruellest that flesh is heir to. Her heart ached for Godfrey.

When the Professor had been warmed and comforted by a good dinner, he lit a cigar and sat down before the hearth to read. After a while his wife saw that the book had slid to his knee, and he was looking into the fire. Studying his dark profile, she noticed that the corners of his funny eyebrows rose, as if he were amused by something.

"What are you thinking about, Godfrey?" she said presently. "Just then you were smiling—quite agreeably!"

"I was thinking," he answered absently, "about Euripides; how, when he was an old man, he went and lived in a cave by the sea, and it was thought queer, at the time. It seems that houses had become insupportable to him. I wonder whether it was because he had observed women so closely all his life."

The month of March was the dreariest and bleakest of the year in Hamilton, and Louie strove to brighten it by opening a discussion of plans for the summer. He had been hinting for some time that he had a very attractive project up his sleeve, and though he had not succeeded in keeping it from Mrs. St. Peter, he said nothing to the Professor until one night when they were dining at the Marselluses'. All through dinner Louie kept reminding them of the specialties of this and that Paris restaurant, so that St. Peter was not altogether unprepared.

As they left the dining-room, Louie burst out with it. He and Rosamond were to take Doctor and Mrs. St. Peter to France for the summer. Louie had decided upon the dates, the boat, the itinerary; he was intoxicated with the pleasure of planning.

"Understand," he said, "it is to be our excursion, from Hamilton back to Hamilton. We'll travel in the most ample comfort, but not in magnificence. We'll go down to Biarritz for a little fashionable life, and stop at Marseilles to see your foster-brother, Charles Thierault. The rest of the summer we'll lead a scholarly life in Paris. I have my own reasons for wishing you to go along, Professor. The pleasure of your company would be quite enough, but I have also other reasons. I want to see the intellectual side of Paris, and to meet some of the savants and men of letters whom you know. What a shame Gaston Paris is not living! We could very nicely make up a little party at Lapérouse for him. But there are others."

Mrs. St. Peter developed the argument. "Yes, Louie, you and Godfrey can lunch with the scholars while Rosamond and I are shopping."

Marsellus looked alarmed. "Not at all, Dearest! It's to be understood that I always shop with you. I adore the shops in Paris. Besides, we shall want you with us when we lunch with celebrities. When was a savant, and a Frenchman, not eager for the company of two charming ladies at *déjeuner?* And you may have too much of the society of your *sposi;* very nice for you to have variety. You must keep a little engagement book: *Lundi, déjeuner, M. Emile Faguet. Mercredi, diner, M. Anatole France;* and so on."

St. Peter chuckled. "I'm afraid you exaggerate the circumference of my social circle, Louie. I haven't the pleasure of knowing Anatole France."

"No matter; we can have M. Paul Bourget for Wednesday."

"You can help us, too, about finding things for the house, Papa," said Rosamond. "We expect to pick up a good many things. The Thieraults ought to know good shops down in the South, where prices have not gone up."

"I'm afraid the antiquaries are centralized in Paris. I

never saw anything very interesting in Lyons or the Midi. However, they may exist."

"Charles Thierault is still interested in a shipping-line that runs to the City of Mexico, isn't he? He could perfectly well send our purchases from Marseilles to the City of Mexico for us. They would go in without duty, and Louie thinks he can get them across the border as household goods."

"That sounds practicable, Rosie. It might be managed."

Marsellus laughed and patted his wife's hand. "Oh-ho, *cher Papa*, you haven't begun to find how practical we can be!"

"Well, Louie, it's a tempting idea, and I'll think it over. I'll see whether I can arrange my work." St. Peter knew at that moment that he would never be one of this light-hearted expedition, and he hated himself for the ungracious drawing-back that he felt in the region of his diaphragm.

The family discussed their summer plans all evening. Louie wanted to write at once for rooms at the Meurice, but Mrs. St. Peter ruled it out as too expensive.

That night, after he was in bed, St. Peter tried in vain to justify himself in his inevitable refusal. He liked Paris, and he liked Louie. But one couldn't do one's own things in another person's way; selfish or not, that was the truth. Besides, he would not be needed. He could trust Louie to take every care of Lillian, and nobody could please her more than her son-in-law. *Beaux-fils,* apparently, were meant by Providence to take the husband's place when husbands had ceased to be lovers. Marsellus never forgot one of the hundred foolish little attentions that Lillian loved. Best of all, he admired her extravagantly, her distinction was priceless to him. Many people admired her, but Louie more than most. That worldliness, that willingness to get the most out of occasions and people, which had developed so strongly in Lillian in the last few years, seemed to Louie as natural and proper as it seemed unnatural to Godfrey. It was an element that had always been in Lillian, and as long as it resulted in mere fastidiousness, was not a means to an end, St. Peter had liked it, too. He knew it was due to this worldliness, even more than to the fact that his wife had a little money of her own, that she and his daughters had never been drab and a little pathetic, like some of the faculty women. They hadn't much, but they were never absurd. They never made shabby compromises. If they couldn't get the right thing, they went without. Usually they had the right thing, and it got paid for, somehow. He couldn't say they were extravagant; the old house had been funny and bare enough, but there were no ugly things in it.

Since Rosamond's marriage to Marsellus, both she and her mother had changed bewilderingly in some respects—changed and hardened. But Louie, who had done the damage, had not damaged himself. It was to him that one appealed,—for Augusta, for Professor

Crane, for the bruised feelings of people less fortunate. It was less because of Louie than for any other reason that he would refuse this princely invitation.

He could get out of it without hurting anybody— though he knew Louie would be sorry. He could simply insist that he must work, and that he couldn't work away from his old study. There were some advantages about being a writer of histories. The desk was a shelter one could hide behind, it was a hole one could creep into.

When St. Peter told his family of his decision, Louie was disappointed; but he was respectful, and readily conceded that the Professor's first duty was to his work. Rosamond was incredulous and piqued; she didn't see how he could be so ungenerous as to spoil an arrangement which would give pleasure to everyone concerned. His wife looked at him with thoughtful disbelief.

When they were alone together, she approached the matter more directly than was her wont nowadays.

"Godfrey," she said slowly and sadly, "I wonder what it is that makes you draw away from your family. Or who it is."

"My dear, are you going to be jealous?"

"I wish I were going to be. I'd much rather see you foolish about some woman than becoming lonely and inhuman."

"Well, the habit of living with ideas grows on one,

I suppose, just as inevitably as the more cheerful habit of living with various ladies. There's something to be said for both."

"I think your ideas were best when you were your most human self."

St. Peter sighed. "I can't contradict you there. But I must go on as I can. It is not always May."

"You are not old enough for the pose you take. That's what puzzles me. For so many years you never seemed to grow at all older, though I did. Two years ago you were an impetuous young man. Now you save yourself in everything. You're naturally warm and affectionate; all at once you begin shutting yourself away from everybody. I don't think you'll be happier for it." Up to this point she had been lecturing him. Now she suddenly crossed the room and sat down on the arm of his chair, looking into his face and twisting up the ends of his military eyebrows with her thumb and middle finger. "Why is it, Godfrey? I can't see any change in your face, though I watch you so closely. It's in your mind, in your mood. Something has come over you. Is it merely that you know too much, I wonder? Too much to be happy? You were always the wisest person in the world. What is it, can't you tell me?"

"I can't altogether tell myself, Lillian. It's not wholly a matter of the calendar. It's the feeling that I've put a great deal behind me, where I can't go back to it again—and I don't really wish to go back. The way would be too long and too fatiguing. Perhaps, for a home-staying man, I've lived pretty hard. I wasn't willing to slight anything—you, or my desk, or my students. And now I seem to be tremendously tired. One pays, coming or going. A man has got only just so much in him; when it's gone he slumps. Even the first Napoleon did." They both laughed. That was an old joke—the Professor's darkest secret. At the font he had been christened Napoleon Godfrey St. Peter. There had always been a Napoleon in the family, since a remote grandfather got his discharge from the Grande Armée. Godfrey had abbreviated his name in Kansas, and even his daughters didn't know what it had been originally.

"I think, you know," he told his wife as he rose to go to bed, "that I'll get my second wind. But for the present I don't want anything very stimulating. Paris is too beautiful, and too full of memories."

One Saturday morning in the spring, when the Professor was at work in the old house, he heard energetic footsteps running up the uncarpeted stairway. Louie's voice called:

"*Cher Papa,* shall I disturb you too much?"

St. Peter rose and opened to him. Louie was wearing his golf stockings, and a purple jacket with a fur collar.

"No, I'm not going golfing. I changed my mind, but didn't have time to change my clothes. I want you to take a run out along the lake-shore with us. Rosie is going to lunch with some friends at the Country Club. We'll have a drive with her, and then drop her there. It's a glorious day." Louie's keen, interested eye ran about the shabby little room. He chuckled. "The old bear, he just likes his old den, doesn't he? I can readily understand. Your children were born here. Not your daughters—your sons, your splendid Spanish-adventurer sons! I'm proud to be related to them, even by marriage. And your blanket, surely that's a Spanish touch!" Louie pounced upon the purple blanket, threw it across his chest, and, moving aside the wire lady, studied himself in Augusta's glass. "And a very proper dressing-gown it would make for Louie, wouldn't it?"

"It was Outland's—a precious possession. His lost chum brought it up from Mexico."

"Was it Outland's, indeed?" Louie stroked it and regarded it in the glass with increased admiration. "I can never forgive destiny that I hadn't the chance to know that splendid fellow."

The Professor's eyebrows rose in puzzled interrogation. "It might have been awkward—about Rosie, you know."

"I never think of him as a rival," said Louie, throwing back the blanket with a wide gesture. "I think of him as a brother, an adored and gifted brother."

Half an hour later they were spinning along through the country, just coming green, Rosamond and her father on the back seat, Louie facing them. It struck the Professor that Louie had something on his mind; his restless bright eyes watched his wife narrowly, as if to seize an opportune moment.

"You know, Doctor," he said presently, "we've decided to give up our house before we go abroad, and cut off the rent. We'll move the books and pictures up to Outland (and our wedding presents, of course), and the silver we'll put in the bank. There won't be much of our present furniture that we'll need. I wonder if you could use any of it? And it has just occurred to me, Rosie," here he leaned forward and tapped her knee, "that we might ask Scott and Kathleen to come round and select anything they like. No use bothering to sell it, we'd get so little."

Rosamond looked at him in astonishment. It was

very evident they had not discussed anything of this sort before. "Don't be foolish, Louie," she said quietly. "They wouldn't want your things."

"But why not?" he persisted playfully. "They are very nice things. Not right for Outland, but perfectly right for a little house. We chose them with care, and we don't want them going into some dirty second-hand shop."

"They won't have to. We can store them in the attic at Outland, Heaven knows it's big enough! You don't have to do anything with them just now."

"It seems a pity, when somebody might be getting the good of them. I know Scott could do very well with that chiffonier of mine. He admired it greatly, I remember, and said he'd never had one with proper drawers for his shirts."

Rosamond's lip curled.

"Don't look like that, Rosie! It's naughty. Stop it!" Louie reached forward and shook her gently by the elbows. "And how can you be sure the McGregors wouldn't like our things, when you've never asked them? What positive ideas she does get into her head!"

"They wouldn't want them because they are ours, yours and mine, if you will have it," she said coldly, drawing away from him.

Louie sank back into his seat and gave it up. "Why do you think such naughty things? I don't believe it, you know! You are so touchy. Scott and Kitty may be a little stand-offish, but it might very possibly make

them feel better if you went at them nicely about this."
He rallied and began to coax again. "She's got it into
her head that the McGregors have a grudge, Doctor.
There's nothing to it."

Rosamond had grown quite pale. Her upper lip, that
was so like her mother's when she was affable, so much
harder when she was not, came down like a steel curtain. "I happen to know, Louie, that Scott blackballed
you for the Arts and Letters. You can call that a grudge
or not, as you please."

Marsellus was visibly shaken. He looked sad. "Well,
if he did, it wasn't very nice of him, certainly. But are
you sure, Rosie? Rumours do go about, and people like
to stir up family differences."

"It isn't people, and it's not rumour. I know it positively. Kathleen's best friend told me."

Louie lay back and shook with laughter. "Oh, the
ladies, the ladies! What they do to each other, Professor!"

St. Peter was very uncomfortable. "I don't think I'd
accept such evidence, Rosamond. I don't believe it of
Scott, and I think Louie has the right idea. People are
like children, and Scott's poor and proud. I think
Louie's chiffonier would go to his heart, if Louie offered it to him. I'm afraid you wouldn't do it very
graciously."

"Professor, I'll go to McGregor's office and put it up
to him. If he scorns it, so much the worse for him.
He'll lose a very handy piece of furniture."

Rosamond's paleness changed to red. Fortunately they were spinning over the gravel loops that led through shaven turf to the Country Club. "You can do as you like with your own things, Louie. But I don't want any of mine in the McGregors' bungalow. I know Scott's brand of humour too well, and the kind of jokes that would be made about them."

The car stopped. Louie sprang out and gave his arm to his wife. He walked up the steps to the door with her, and his back expressed such patient, protecting kindness that the Professor bit his lower lip with indignation. Louie came back looking quite grey and tired, and sank into the seat beside the Professor with a sadder-and-wiser smile.

"Louie," St. Peter spoke with deep feeling, "do you happen to have read a novel of Henry James, *The American?* There's a rather nice scene in it, in which a young Frenchman, hurt in a duel, apologizes for the behaviour of his family. I'd like to do something of the sort. I apologize to you for Rosamond, and for Scott, if he has done such a mean thing."

Louie's downcast face brightened at once. He squeezed the Professor's arm warmly. "Oh, *that's* all right, sir! As for Scott, I can understand. He was the first son of the family, and he was the whole thing. Then I came along, a stranger, and carried off Rosie, and this patent began to pay so well—it's enough to make any man jealous, and he a Scotchman! But I think Scott will come around in the end; people usually do, if you treat them well, and I mean to. I like the fellow. As for Rosamond, you mustn't give that a thought. I love her when she's naughty. She's a bit unreasonable sometimes, but I'm always hoping for a period of utter, of fantastic unreasonableness, which will be the beginning of a great happiness for us all."

"Louie, you are magnanimous and magnificent!" murmured his vanquished father-in-law.

Lillian and the Marselluses sailed for France early in May. The Professor, left alone, had plenty of time to spray his rose-vines, and his garden had never been so beautiful as it was that June. After his university duties were over, he smuggled his bed and clothing back to the old house and settled down to a leisurely bachelor life. He realized that he ought to be getting to work. The garden, in which he sat all day, was no longer a valid excuse to keep him from his study. But the task that awaited him up there was difficult. It was a little thing, but one of those little things at which the hand becomes self-conscious, feels itself stiff and clumsy.

It was his plan to give part of this summer to Tom Outland's diary—to edit and annotate it for publication. The bother was that he must write an introduction. The diary covered only about six months of the boy's life, a summer he spent on the Blue Mesa, and in it there was almost nothing about Tom himself. To mean anything, it must be prefaced by a sketch of Outland, and some account of his later life and achievements. To write of his scientific work would be comparatively easy. But that was not all the story; his was a many-sided mind, though a simple and straightforward personality.

Of course Mrs. St. Peter had insisted that he was not altogether straightforward; but that was merely because he was not altogether consistent. As an investigator he was clear-sighted and hard-headed; but in personal relations he was apt to be exaggerated and quixotic. He idealized the people he loved and paid his devoir to the ideal rather than to the individual, so that his behaviour was sometimes a little too exalted for the circumstances—"chivalry of the cinema," Lillian used to say. One of his sentimental superstitions was that he must never on any account owe any material advantage to his friends, that he must keep affection and advancement far apart, as if they were chemicals that would disintegrate each other. St. Peter thought this the logical result of Tom's strange bringing-up and his early associations. There is, he knew, this dream of self-sacrificing friendship and disinterested love down among the day-labourers, the men who run the railroad trains and boats and reapers and thrashers and mine-drills of the world. And Tom had brought it along to the university, where advancement through personal influence was considered honourable.

It was not until Outland was a senior that Lillian began to be jealous of him. He had been almost a member of the family for two years, and she had never found fault with the boy. But after the Professor began to take Tom up to the study and talk over his work with him, began to make a companion of him, then Mrs. St. Peter withdrew her favour. She could change like that; friendship was not a matter of habit with her. And when she was through with anyone, she of course found reasons for her fickleness. Tom, she reminded her husband, was far from frank, though he had such an open manner. He had been consistently reserved about his own affairs, and she could not believe the facts he withheld were altogether creditable. They had always known he had a secret, something to do with the mysterious Rodney Blake and the bank account in New Mexico upon which he was not at liberty to draw. The young man must have felt the change in her, for he began that winter to make his work a pretext for coming to the house less often. He and St. Peter now met in the alcove behind the Professor's lecture room at the university.

One Sunday, shortly before Tom's Commencement, he came to the house to ask Rosamond to go to the senior dance with him. The family were having tea in the garden; a few days of intensely warm weather had come on and hurried the roses into bloom. Rosamond happened to ask Tom, who sat in his white flannels, fanning himself with his straw hat, if spring in the South-west was as warm as this.

"Oh, no," he replied. "May is usually chilly down there—bright sun, but a kind of edge in the wind, and cool nights. Last night reminded me of smothery May nights in Washington."

Mrs. St. Peter glanced up. "You mean Washington City? I didn't know you had ever been so far east."

There was no denying that the young man looked

uncomfortable. He frowned and said in a low voice: "Yes, I've been there. I suppose I don't speak of it because I haven't very pleasant recollections of it."

"How long were you there?" his hostess asked.

"A winter and spring, more than six months. Long enough to get very home-sick." He went away almost at once, as if he were afraid of being questioned further.

The subject came up again a few weeks later, however. After Tom's graduation, two courses were open to him. He was offered an instructorship, with a small salary, in the Physics department under Dr. Crane, and a graduate scholarship at Johns Hopkins University. St. Peter strongly urged him to accept the latter. One evening when the family were discussing Tom's prospects, the Professor summed up all the reasons why he ought to go to Baltimore and work in the laboratory made famous by Dr. Rowland. He assured him, moreover, that he would find the atmosphere of an old Southern city delightful.

"Yes, I know something about the atmosphere," Tom broke out at last. "It is delightful, but it's all wrong for me. It discourages me dreadfully. I used to go over there when I was in Washington, and it always made me blue. I don't believe I could ever work there."

"But can you trust a child's impressions to guide you now, in such an important decision?" asked Mrs. St. Peter gravely.

"I wasn't a child, Mrs. St. Peter. I was as much grown up as I am now—older, in some ways. It was only about a year before I came here."

"But, Tom, you were on the section gang that year! Why do you mix us all up?" Kathleen caught his hand and squeezed the knuckles together, as she did when she wanted to punish him.

"Well, maybe it was two years before. It doesn't matter. It was long enough to count for two ordinary years," he muttered abstractedly.

Again he went away abruptly, and a few days later he told St. Peter that he had definitely accepted the instructorship under Crane, and would stay on in Hamilton.

During that summer after Outland's graduation, St. Peter got to know all there was behind his reserve. Mrs. St. Peter and the two girls were in Colorado, and the Professor was alone in the house, writing on volumes three and four of his history. Tom was carrying on some experiments of his own, over in the Physics laboratory. He and St. Peter were often together in the evening, and on fine afternoons they went swimming. Every Saturday the Professor turned his house over to the cleaning-woman, and he and Tom went to the lake and spent the day in his sail-boat.

It was just the sort of summer St. Peter liked, if he had to be in Hamilton at all. He was his own cook, and had laid in a choice assortment of cheeses and light Italian wines from a discriminating importer in Chicago. Every morning before he sat down at his desk he took a walk to the market and had his pick of the fruits and salads. He dined at eight o'clock. When he cooked a fine leg of lamb, *saignant,* well rubbed with garlic before it went into the pan, then he asked Outland to dinner. Over a dish of steaming asparagus, swathed in a napkin to keep it hot, and a bottle of sparkling Asti, they talked and watched night fall in the garden. If the evening happened to be rainy or chilly, they sat inside and read Lucretius.

It was on one of those rainy nights, before the fire in the dining-room, that Tom at last told the story he had always kept back. It was nothing very incriminating, nothing very remarkable; a story of youthful defeat, the sort of thing a boy is sensitive about—until he grows older.

BOOK TWO

Tom Outland's Story

O N E

The thing that side-tracked me and made me so late coming to college was a somewhat unusual accident, or string of accidents. It began with a poker game, when I was a call boy in Pardee, New Mexico.

One cold, clear night in the fall I started out to hunt up a freight crew that was to go out soon after midnight. It was just after pay day, and one of the fellows had tipped me off that there would be a poker game going on in the card-room behind the Ruby Light saloon. I knew most of my crew would be there, except Conductor Willis, who had a sick baby at home. The front windows were dark, of course. I went up the back alley, through a tumble-down ice house and a court, into a 'dobe room that didn't open into the saloon proper at all. It was crowded, and hot and stuffy enough. There were six or seven in the game, and a crowd of fellows were standing about the walls, rubbing the white-wash off on to their coat shoulders. There was a bird-cage hanging in one window, covered with an old flannel shirt, but the canary had wakened up and was singing away for dear life. He was a beautiful singer—an old Mexican had trained him—and he was one of the attractions of the place.

I happened along when a jack-pot was running. Two of the fellows I'd come for were in it, and they naturally wanted to finish the hand. I stood by the door with my watch, keeping time for them. Among the players I saw two sheep men who always liked a lively game, and one of the bystanders told me you had to buy a hundred dollars' worth of chips to get in that night. The crowd was fussing about one fellow, Rodney Blake, who had come in from his engine without cleaning up. That wasn't customary; the minute a man got in from his run, he took a bath, put on citizen's clothes, and went to a barber. This Blake was a new fireman on our division. He'd come up town in his greasy overalls and sweaty blue shirt, with his face streaked up with smoke. He'd been drinking; he smelled of it, and his eyes were out of focus. All the other men were clean and freshly shaved, and they were sore at Blake— said his hands were so greasy they marked the cards. Some of them wanted to put him out of the game, but he was a big, heavy-built fellow, and nobody wanted to be the man to do it. It didn't please them any better when he took the jack-pot.

I got my two men and hurried them out, and two others from the row along the wall took their places. One of the chaps who left with me asked me to go up to his house and get his grip with his work clothes. He'd lost every cent of his pay cheque and didn't want to face his wife. I asked him who was winning.

"Blake. The dirty boomer's been taking everything. But the fellows will clean him out before morning."

About two o'clock, when my work for that night was over and I was going home to sleep, I just dropped in at the card-room to see how things had come out. The game was breaking up. Since I left them at midnight, they had changed to stud poker, and Blake, the fireman, had cleaned everybody out. He was cashing in his chips when I came in. The bank was a little short, but Blake made no fuss about it. He had something over sixteen hundred dollars lying on the table before him in bank-notes and gold. Some of the crowd were insulting him, trying to get him into a fight and loot him. He paid no attention and began to put the money away, not looking at anybody. The bills he folded and put inside the band of his hat. He filled his overalls pockets with the gold, and swept the rest of it into his big red neckerchief.

I'd been interested in this fellow ever since he came on our division; he was close-mouthed and unfriendly. He was one of those fellows with a settled, mature body and a young face, such as you often see among working-men. There was something calm, and sarcastic, and mocking about his expression—that, too, you often see among working-men. When he had put all his money away, he got up and walked toward the door without a word, without saying good-night to anybody.

"Manners of a hog, and a dirty hog!" little Barney Shea yelled after him. Blake's back was just in the doorway; he hitched up one shoulder, but didn't turn or make a sound.

I slipped out after him and followed him down the street. His walk was unsteady, and the gold in his baggy overalls pockets clinked with every step he took. I ran a little way and caught up with him. "What are you going to do with all that money, Blake?" I asked him.

"Lose it, to-morrow night. I'm no hog for money. Damned barber-pole dudes!"

I thought I'd better follow him home. I knew he lodged with an old Mexican woman, in the yellow quarter, behind the round-house. His room opened on to the street, by a sky-blue door. He went in, didn't strike a light or make a stab at undressing, but threw himself just as he was on the bed and went to sleep. His hat stuck between the iron rods of the bed-head, the gold ran out of his pockets and rolled over the bare floor in the dark.

I struck a match and lit a candle. The bed took up half the room; on the dresser was a grip with his clean clothes in it, just as he'd brought it in from his run. I took out the clothes and began picking up the money; got the bills out of his hat, emptied his pockets, and collected the coins that lay in the hollow of the bed about his hips, and put it all into the grip. Then I blew out the light and sat down to listen. I trusted all the boys who were at the Ruby Light that night, except Barney Shea. He might try to pull something off on a stranger, down in Mexican town. We had a quiet night, however, and a cold one. I found Blake's winter over-coat hanging on the wall and wrapped up in it. I wasn't a bit sorry when the roosters began to crow and the dogs began barking all over Mexican town. At last the sun came up and turned the desert and the 'dobe town red in a minute. I began to shake the man on the bed. Waking men who didn't want to get up was part of my job, and I didn't let up on him until I had him on his feet.

"Hello, kid, come to call me?"

I told him I'd come to call him to a Harvey House breakfast. "You owe me a good one. I brought you home last night."

"Sure, I'm glad to have company. Wait till I wash up a bit." He took his soap and towel and comb and went out into the patio, a neat little sanded square with flowers and vines all around, and washed at the trough under the pump. Then he called me to come and pump water on his head. After he'd stood the gush of cold water for a few seconds, he straightened up with his teeth chattering.

"That ought to get the whisky out of a fellow's head, oughtn't it? Felt good, Tom." Presently he began feeling his side pockets. "Was I dreaming something, or did I take a string of jack-pots last night?"

"The money's in your grip," I told him. "You don't deserve it, for you were too drunk to take care of it. I had to come after you and pick it up out of the mud."

"All right. I'll go halvers. Easy come, easy go."

I told him I didn't want anything off him but breakfast, and I wanted that pretty soon.

"Go easy, son. I've got to change my shirt. This one's wet."

"It's worse than wet. You oughtn't to go up town without changing. You're a stranger here, and it makes a bad impression."

He shrugged his shoulders and looked superior. He had a square-built, honest face and steady eyes that didn't carry a cynical expression very well. I knew he was a decent chap, though he'd been drinking and acting ugly ever since he'd been on our division.

After breakfast we went out and sat in the sun at a place where the wooden sidewalk ran over a sand gully and made a sort of bridge. I had a long talk with him. I was carrying the grip with his winnings in it, and I finally persuaded him to go with me to the bank. We put every cent of it into a savings account that he couldn't touch for a year.

From that night Blake and I were fast friends. He was the sort of fellow who can do anything for somebody else, and nothing for himself. There are lots like that among working-men. They aren't trained by success to a sort of systematic selfishness. Rodney had been unlucky in personal relations. He'd run away from home when he was a kid because his mother married again—a man who had been paying attention to her while his father was still alive. He got engaged to a girl down on the Southern Pacific, and she double-crossed him, as he said. He went to Old Mexico and let his friends put all his savings into an oil well, and they skinned him. What he needed was a pal, a straight fellow to give an account to. I was ten years younger, and that was an advantage. He liked to be an older brother. I suppose the fact that I was a kind of stray and had no family, made it easier for him to unbend to me. He surely got to think a lot of me, and I did of him. It was that winter I had pneumonia. Mrs. O'Brien couldn't do much for me; she was overworked, poor woman, with a houseful of children. Blake took me down to his room, and he and the old Mexican woman nursed me. He ought to have had boys of his own to look after. Nature's full of such substitutions, but they always seem to me sad, even in botany.

I wasn't able to be about until spring, and then the doctor and Father Duchene said I must give up night work and live in the open all summer. Before I knew anything about it, Blake had thrown up his job on the Santa Fé, and got a berth for him and me with the Sitwell Cattle Company. Jonas Sitwell was one of the biggest cattle men in our part of New Mexico. Roddy and I were to ride the range with a bunch of grass cattle all summer, then take them down to a winter camp on the Cruzados river and keep them on pasture until spring.

We went out about the first of May, and joined our cattle twenty miles south of Pardee, down toward the Blue Mesa. The Blue Mesa was one of the landmarks we always saw from Pardee—landmarks mean so much in a flat country. To the northwest, over toward Utah, we had the Mormon Buttes, three sharp blue peaks that always sat there. The Blue Mesa was south of us, and was much stronger in colour, almost purple. People said the rock itself had a deep purplish cast. It looked, from our town, like a naked blue rock set down alone in the plain, almost square, except that the top was higher at one end. The old settlers said nobody had ever climbed it, because the sides were so steep and the Cruzados river wound round it at one end and under-cut it.

Blake and I knew that the Sitwell winter camp was down on the Cruzados river, directly under the mesa, and all summer long, while we drifted about with our cattle from one water-hole to another, we planned how we were going to climb the mesa and be the first men up there. After supper, when we lit our pipes and watched the sunset, climbing the mesa was our staple topic of conversation. Our job was a cinch; the actual work wouldn't have kept one man busy. The Sitwell people were good to their hands. John Rapp, the fore-man, came along once a month in his spring-wagon, to see how the cattle were doing and to bring us supplies and bundles of old newspapers.

Blake was a conscientious reader of newspapers. He always wanted to know what was going on in the world, though most of it displeased him. He brooded on the great injustices of his time; the hanging of the Anar-chists in Chicago, which he could just remember, and the Dreyfus case. We had long arguments about what we read in the papers, but we never quarrelled. The only trouble I had with Blake was in getting to do my share of the work. He made my health a pretext for taking all the heavy chores, long after I was as well as he was. I'd brought my Cæsar along, and had promised Father Duchene to read a hundred lines a day. Blake saw that I did it—made me translate the dull stuff aloud to him. He said if I once knew Latin, I wouldn't have to work with my back all my life like a burro. He had great respect for education, but he believed it was some kind of hocus-pocus that enabled a man to live without work. We had *Robinson Crusoe* with us, and Roddy's favourite book, *Gulliver's Travels,* which he never tired of.

Late in October, Rapp, the foreman, came along to accompany us down to the winter camp. Blake stayed with the cattle about fifteen miles to the east, where the grass was still good, and Rapp and I went down to air out the cabin and stow away our winter supplies.

TWO

The cabin stood in a little grove of piñons, about thirty yards back from the Cruzados river, facing south and sheltered on the north by a low hill. The grama grass grew right up to the door-step, and the rabbits were running about and the grasshoppers hitting the door when we pulled up and looked at the place. There was no litter around, it was as clean as a prairie-dog's house. No outbuildings, except a shed for our horses. The hill-side behind was sandy and covered with tall clumps of deer-horn cactus, but there was nothing but grass to the south, with streaks of bright yellow rabbit-brush. Along the river the cottonwoods and quaking asps had already turned gold. Just across from us, over-hanging us, indeed, stood the mesa, a pile of purple rock, all broken out with red sumach and yellow as-pens up in the high crevices of the cliffs. From the cabin, night and day, you could hear the river, where it made a bend round the foot of the mesa and churned over the rocks. It was the sort of place a man would like to stay in forever.

I helped Rapp open the wooden shutters and sweep out the cabin. We put clean blankets on the bunks, and stowed away bacon and coffee and canned stuff on the shelves behind the cook-stove. I confess I looked forward to cooking on an iron stove with four holes. Rapp explained to me that Blake and I wouldn't be able to enjoy all this luxury together for a time. He wanted the herd kept some distance to the north as long as the grass held out up there, and Roddy and I could take turn about, one camping near the cattle and one sleeping in a bed.

"There's not pasture enough down here to take them through a long winter," he said, "and it's safest to keep them grazing up north while you can. Besides, if you bring them down here while the weather's so warm, they get skittish, and that mesa over there makes trouble. They swim the river and bolt into the mesa, and that's the last you ever see of them. We've lost a lot of critters that way. The mesa has been populated by runaways from our herd, till now there's a fine bunch of wild cattle up there. When the wind's right, our cows over here get the scent of them and make a break for the river. You'll have to watch 'em close when you bring 'em down."

I asked him whether nobody had ever gone over to get the lost cattle out.

Rapp glared at me. "Out of that mesa? Nobody has ever got into it yet. The cliffs are like the base of a monument, all the way round. The only way into it is through that deep canyon that opens on the water level, just where the river makes the bend. You can't get in by that, because the river's too deep to ford and too swift to swim. Oh, I suppose a horse could swim it, if cattle can, but I don't want to be the man to try."

I remarked that I had had my eye on the mesa all summer and meant to climb it.

"Not while you're working for the Sitwell Company, you don't! If you boys try any nonsense of that sort, I'll fire you quick. You'd break your bones and lose the herd for us. You have to watch them close to keep them from going over, I tell you. If it wasn't for that mesa, this would be the best winter range in all New Mexico."

After the foreman left us, we settled down to easy living and fine weather; blue and gold days, and clear, frosty nights. We kept the cattle off to the north and east and alternated in taking charge of them. One man was with the herd while the other got his sleep and did the cooking at the cabin. The mesa was our only neighbour, and the closer we got to it, the more tantalizing it was. It was no longer a blue, featureless lump, as it had been from a distance. Its sky-line was like the profile of a big beast lying down; the head to the north, higher than the flanks around which the river curved. The north end we could easily believe impassable—sheer cliffs that fell from the summit to the plain, more than a thousand feet. But the south flank, just across the river from us, looked accessible by way of the deep canyon that split the bulk in two, from the top rim to the river, then wound back into the solid cube so that it was invisible at a distance, like a mouse track winding into a big cheese. This canyon didn't break the solid outline of the mesa, and you had to be close to see

170

that it was there at all. We faced the mesa on its short-est side; it was only about three miles long from north to south, but east and west it measured nearly twice that distance. Whether the top was wooded we couldn't see—it was too high above us; but the cliffs and canyon on the river side were fringed with beautiful growth, groves of quaking asps and piñons and a few dark ce-dars, perched up in the air like the hanging gardens of Babylon. At certain hours of the day, those cedars, growing so far up on the rocks, took on the bluish tint of the cliffs themselves.

It was light up there long before it was with us. When I got up at daybreak and went down to the river to get water, our camp would be cold and grey, but the mesa top would be red with sunrise, and all the slim cedars along the rocks would be gold—metallic, like tarnished gold-foil. Some mornings it would loom up above the dark river like a blazing volcanic moun-tain. It shortened our days, too, considerably. The sun got behind it early in the afternoon, and then our camp would lie in its shadow. After a while the sunset colour would begin to stream up from behind it. Then the mesa was like one great ink-black rock against a sky on fire.

No wonder the thing bothered us and tempted us; it was always before us, and was always changing. Black thunder-storms used to roll up from behind it and pounce on us like a panther without warning. The lightning would play round it and jab into it so that we were always expecting it would fire the brush. I've never heard thunder so loud as it was there. The cliffs threw it back at us, and we thought the mesa itself, though it seemed so solid, must be full of deep canyons and caverns, to account for the prolonged growl and rumble that followed every crash of thunder. After the burst in the sky was over, the mesa went on sounding like a drum, and seemed itself to be muttering and making noises.

One afternoon I was out hunting turkeys. Just as the sun was getting low, I came through a sea of rabbit-brush, still yellow, and the horizontal rays of light, playing into it, brought out the contour of the ground with great distinctness. I noticed a number of straight mounds, like plough furrows, running from the river inland. It was too late to examine them. I cut a scrub willow and stuck a stake into one of the ridges, to mark it. The next day I took a spade down to the plantation of rabbit-brush and dug around in the sandy soil. I came upon an old irrigation main, unmistakable, lined with hard smooth cobbles and 'dobe cement, with sluices where the water had been let out into trenches. Along these ditches I turned up some pieces of pottery, all of it broken, and arrow-heads, and a very neat, well-finished stone pick-ax.

That night I didn't go back to the cabin, but took my specimens out to Blake, who was still north with the cattle. Of course, we both knew there had been Indians all over this country, but we felt sure that Indians hadn't used stone tools for a long while back. There must have been a colony of pueblo Indians here in ancient times: fixed residents, like the Taos Indians and the Hopis, not wanderers like the Navajos.

To people off alone, as we were, there is something stirring about finding evidences of human labour and care in the soil of an empty country. It comes to you as a sort of message, makes you feel differently about the ground you walk over every day. I liked the winter range better than any place I'd ever been in. I never came out of the cabin door in the morning to go after water that I didn't feel fresh delight in our snug quarters and the river and the old mesa up there, with its top burning like a bonfire. I wanted to see what it was like on the other side, and very soon I took a day off and forded the river where it was wide and shallow, north of our camp. I rode clear around the mesa, until I met the river again where it flowed under the south flank.

On that ride I got a better idea of its actual structure. All the way round were the same precipitous cliffs of hard blue rock, but in places it was mixed with a much softer stone. In these soft streaks there were deep dry watercourses which could certainly be climbed as far as they went, but nowhere did they reach to the top of the mesa. The top seemed to be one great slab of very hard rock, lying on the mixed mass of the base like the top of an old-fashioned marble table. The channels worn out by water ran for hundreds of feet up the cliffs, but always stopped under this great rim rock, which projected out over the erosions like a granite shelf. Evidently, it was because of this unbroken top layer that the butte was inaccessible. I rode back to camp that night, convinced that if we ever climbed it, we must take the route the cattle took, through the river and up the one canyon that broke down to water-level.

THREE

We brought the bunch of cattle down to the winter range in the latter part of November. Early in December the foreman came along with generous provisions for Christmas. This time he brought with him a supercargo, a pitiful wreck of an old man he had picked up at Tarpin, the railroad town thirty miles north-east of us, where the Sitwells bought their supplies. This old man was a castaway Englishman, Henry Atkins by name. He had been a valet, and a hospital orderly, and a cook, and for many years was a table steward on the Anchor Line. Lately he had been cooking for a sheep outfit that were grazing in the cattle country, where they weren't wanted. They had done something shady and had to get out in a hurry. They dropped old Henry at Tarpin, where he soon drank up all his wages. When Rapp picked him up there, he was living on hand-outs.

"I've told him we can't pay him anything," Rapp explained. "But if he wants to stay here and cook for you boys till I make my next trip, he'll have plenty to eat and a roof over him. He was sleeping in the livery stable in Tarpin. He says he's a good cook, and I thought he might liven things up for you at Christmas time. He won't bother you, he's not got any of the mean ways of a bum—I know a bum when I see one. Next time I come down I'll bring him some old clothes from the ranch, and you can fire him if you want to.

All his baggage is that newspaper bundle, and there's nothing in it but shoes—a pair of patent leathers and a pair of sneakers. The important thing is, never, on any account, go off skylarking, you two, and leave him with the cattle. Not for an hour, mind you. He ain't strong enough, and he's got no head."

Life was a holiday for Blake and me after we got old Henry. He was a wonderful cook and a good house-keeper. He kept that cabin shining like a playhouse; used to dress it all out with piñon boughs, and trimmed the kitchen shelves with newspapers cut in fancy patterns. He had learned to make up cots when he was a hospital orderly, and he made our bunks feel like a Harvey House bed. To this day that's the best I can say for any bed. And he was such a polite, mannerly old boy; simple and kind as a child. I used to wonder how anybody so innocent and defenceless had managed to get along at all, to keep alive for nearly seventy years in as hard a world as this. Anybody could take advantage of him. He held no grudge against any of the people who had misused him. He loved to tell about the celebrated people he'd been steward to, and the liberal tips they had given him. There with us, where he couldn't get at whisky, he was a model of good behaviour. "Drink is me weakness, you might say," he occasionally remarked apologetically. He shaved every morning and was as clean as a pin. We got to be down-right fond of him, and the three of us made a happy family.

Ever since we'd brought our herd down to the winter camp, the wild cattle on the mesa were more in evidence. They came down to the river to drink oftener, and loitered about, grazing in that low canyon so much that we began to call it Cow Canyon. They were fine-looking beasts, too. One could see they had good pasture up there. Henry had a theory that we ought to be able to entice them over to our side with salt. He wanted to kill one for beef-steaks. Soon after he joined us we lost two cows. Without warning they bolted into the mesa, as the foreman had said. After that we watched the herd closer; but a few days before Christmas, when Blake was off hunting and I was on duty, four fine young steers sneaked down to the water's edge through the brush, and before I knew it they were swimming the river—seemed to do it with no trouble at all. They frisked out on the other side, ambled up the canyon, and disappeared. I was furious to have them steal a march on me, and I swore to myself I'd follow them over and drive them back.

The next morning we took the herd a few miles east, to keep them out of mischief. I made some excuse to Blake, cut back to the cabin, and asked Henry to put me up a lunch. I told him my plan, but warned him not to bear tales. If I wasn't home when Blake came in at night, then he could tell him where I'd gone.

Henry went down to the river with me to watch me across. It had grown colder since morning, and looked like snow. The old man was afraid of a storm; said I might get snowed in. But I'd got my nerve up, and I didn't want to put off making a try at it. I strapped my blanket and my lunch on my shoulders, hung my boots around my neck to keep them dry, stuffed my socks inside my hat, and we waded in. My horse took the water without any fuss, though he shivered a good deal. He stepped out very carefully, and when it got too deep for him, he swam without panic. We were carried down-stream a little by the current, but I didn't have to slide off his back. He found bottom after a while, and we easily made a landing. I waved good-bye to Henry on the other side and started up the canyon, running beside my horse to get warm.

The canyon was wide at the water's edge, and though it corkscrewed back into the mesa by abrupt turns, it preserved this open, roomy character. It was, indeed, a very deep valley with gently sloping sides, rugged and rocky, but well grassed. There was a clear trail. Horses have no sense about making a trail, but you can trust cattle to find the easiest possible path and to take the lowest grades. The bluish rock and the sun-tanned grass, under the unusual purple-grey of the sky, gave the whole valley a very soft colour, lavender and pale gold, so that the occasional cedars growing beside the boulders looked black that morning. It may have been the hint of snow in the air, but it seemed to me that I had never breathed in anything that tasted so pure as the air in that valley. It made my mouth and nostrils smart like charged water, seemed to go to my head a little and produce a kind of exaltation. I kept telling myself that it was very different from the air on the other side of the river, though that was pure and uncontaminated enough.

When I had gone up this canyon for a mile or so, I came upon another, opening out to the north—a box canyon, very different in character. No gentle slope there. The walls were perpendicular, where they weren't actually overhanging, and they were anywhere from eight hundred to a thousand feet high, as we afterward found by measurement. The floor of it was a mass of huge boulders, great pieces of rock that had fallen from above ages back, and had been worn round and smooth as pebbles by the long action of water. Many of them were as big as haystacks, yet they lay piled on one another like a load of gravel. There was no footing for my horse among those smooth stones, so I hobbled him and went on alone a little way, just to see what it was like. My eyes were steadily on the ground—a slip of the foot there might cripple one.

It was such rough scrambling that I was soon in a warm sweat under my damp clothes. In stopping to take breath, I happened to glance up at the canyon wall. I wish I could tell you what I saw there, just *as* I saw it, on that first morning, through a veil of lightly falling snow. Far up above me, a thousand feet or so, set in a great cavern in the face of the cliff, I saw a little city of stone, asleep. It was as still as sculpture—and something like that. It all hung together, seemed to have a kind of composition: pale little houses of stone nestling close to one another, perched on top of each other, with flat roofs, narrow windows, straight walls, and in the middle of the group, a round tower.

It was beautifully proportioned, that tower, swelling out to a larger girth a little above the base, then growing slender again. There was something symmetrical and powerful about the swell of the masonry. The tower was the fine thing that held all the jumble of houses together and made them mean something. It was red in colour, even on that grey day. In sunlight it was the colour of winter oak-leaves. A fringe of cedars grew along the edge of the cavern, like a garden. They were the only living things. Such silence and stillness and repose—immortal repose. That village sat looking down into the canyon with the calmness of eternity. The falling snow-flakes, sprinkling the piñons, gave it a special kind of solemnity. I can't describe it. It was more like sculpture than anything else. I knew at once that I had come upon the city of some extinct civilization, hidden away in this inaccessible mesa for centuries, preserved in the dry air and almost perpetual sunlight like a fly in amber, guarded by the cliffs and the river and the desert.

As I stood looking up at it, I wondered whether I ought to tell even Blake about it; whether I ought not to go back across the river and keep that secret as the mesa had kept it. When I at last turned away, I saw still another canyon branching out of this one, and in its wall still another arch, with another group of buildings. The notion struck me like a rifle ball that this mesa had once been like a bee-hive; it was full of little cliff-hung villages, it had been the home of a powerful tribe, a particular civilization.

That night when I got home Blake was on the river-bank waiting for me. I told him I'd rather not talk about my trip until after supper,—that I was beat out. I think he'd meant to upbraid me for sneaking off, but he didn't. He seemed to realize from the first that this was a serious matter to me, and he accepted it in that way.

After supper, when we had lit our pipes, I told Blake and Henry as clearly as I could what it was like over there, and we talked it over. The town in the cliffs explained the irrigation ditches. Like all pueblo Indians, these people had had their farms away from their dwellings. For a stronghold they needed rock, and for farming, soft earth and a water main.

"And this proves," said Roddy, "that there must have been a trail into the mesa at the north end, and that they carried their harvest over by the ford. If this Cow Canyon was the only entrance, they could never have farmed down here." We agreed that he should go over on the first warm day, and try to find a trail up to the Cliff City, as we already called it.

We talked and speculated until after midnight. It was Christmas eve, and Henry said it was but right we should do something out of the ordinary. But after we went to bed, tired as I was, I was unable to sleep. I got up and dressed and put on my overcoat and slipped outside to get sight of the mesa. The wind had come up and was blowing the squall clouds across the sky. The moon was almost full, hanging directly over the mesa, which had never looked so solemn and silent to me before. I wondered how many Christmases had come and gone since that round tower was built. I had been to Acoma and the Hopi villages, but I'd never seen a tower like that one. It seemed to me to mark a difference. I felt that only a strong and aspiring people would have built it, and a people with a feeling for design. That cluster of buildings, in its arch, with the dizzy drop into empty air from its doorways and the wall of cliff above, was as clear in my mind as a picture. By closing my eyes I could see it against the dark, like a magic-lantern slide.

Blake got over the river before New Year's day, but he didn't find any way of getting from the bottom of the box canyon up into the Cliff City. He felt sure that the inhabitants of that sky village had reached it by a trail from the top of the mesa down, not from the bottom of the canyon up. He explored the branch canyons a little, and found four other villages, smaller than the first, placed in similar arches.

These arches we had often seen in other canyons. You can find them in the Grand Canyon, and all along the Rio Grande. Whenever the surface rock is much harder than the rock beneath it, the softer stone begins to crack and crumble with weather just at the line where it meets the hard rim rock. It goes on crumbling and falling away, and in time this wash-out grows to be a spacious cavern. The Cliff City sat in an unusually large cavern. We afterward found that it was three hundred and sixty feet long, and seventy feet high in the centre. The red tower was fifty feet in height.

Blake and I began to make plans. Our engagement with the Sitwell Company terminated in May. When we turned our cattle over to the foreman, we would go into the mesa with what food and tools we could carry, and try to find a trail down the north end, where we were sure there must once have been one. If we could find an easier way to get in and out of the mesa, we would devote the summer, and our winter's wages, to exploring it. From Tarpin, the nearest railroad, we could get supplies and tools, and help if we needed it. We thought we could manage to do the work ourselves if old Henry would stay with us. We didn't want to make our discovery any more public than necessary. We were reluctant to expose those silent and beautiful places to vulgar curiosity. Finally we outlined our plan to Henry, telling him we couldn't promise him regular wages.

"We won't mention it," he said, waving his hand. "I'd ask nothing better than to share your fortunes. In me youth it was me ambition to go to Egypt and see the tombs of the Pharaohs."

"You may get a bad cold going over the river,

Henry," Blake warned him. "It's bad crossing—makes you dizzy when you take to swimming. You have to keep your head."

"I was never seasick in me life," he declared, "and at that, I've helped in the cook's galley on the Anchor Line when she was fair standing on her head. You'll find me strong and active when I'm once broke into the work. I come of an enduring family, though, to be sure, I've abused me constitution somewhat."

Henry liked to talk about his family, and the work they'd done, and the great age to which they lived, and the brandy puddings his mother made. "Eighteen we was in all, when we sat down at table," he would often say with his thin, apologetic smile. "Mother and father, and ten living, and four dead, and two still-born." Roddy and I used to strain our imagination trying to visualize such a family dinner party.

Everything worked out well for us. The foreman showed so much interest in our plans that we told him everything. He insisted that we should stay on at the winter camp as long as we needed a home base, and use up whatever supplies were left. When he paid us off, he sold us our two horses at a very reasonable figure.

FOUR

Blake and I got over to the mesa together for the first time early in May. We carried with us all the food we could, and an ax and spade. It took us several days to find a trail leading from the bottom of the box canyon up to the Cliff City. There were gaps in it; it was broken by ledges too steep for a man to climb. Lying beside one of these, we found an old dried cedar trunk, with toe-notches cut in it. That was a plain suggestion. We felled some trees and threw them up over the gaps in the path. Toward the end of the week, when our provisions were getting low, we made the last lap in our climb, and stepped upon the ledge that was the floor of the Cliff City.

In front of the cluster of buildings, there was an open space, like a court-yard. Along the outer edge of this yard ran a low stone wall. In some places the wall had fallen away from the weather, but the buildings themselves sat so far back under the rim rock that the rain had never beat on them. In thunder-storms I've seen the water come down in sheets over the face of that cavern without a drop touching the village.

The court-yard was not choked by vegetation, for there was no soil. It was bare rock, with a few old, flat-topped cedars growing out of the cracks, and a little pale grass. But everything seemed open and clean, and the stones, I remember, were warm to the touch, smooth and pleasant to feel.

The outer walls of the houses were intact, except where sometimes an outjutting corner had crumbled. They were made of dressed stones, plastered inside and out with 'dobe, and were tinted in light colours, pink and pale yellow and tan. Here and there a cedar log in the ceiling had given way and let the second-story chamber down into the first; except for that, there was little rubbish or disorder. As Blake remarked, wind and sun are good housekeepers.

This village had never been sacked by an enemy, certainly. Inside the little rooms water jars and bowls stood about unbroken, and yucca-fibre mats were on the floors.

We could give only a hurried look over the place, as our food was exhausted, and we had to get back over the river before dark. We went about softly, tried not to disturb anything—even the silence. Besides the tower, there seemed to be about thirty little separate dwellings. Behind the cluster of houses was a kind of back court-yard, running from end to end of the cavern; a long, low, twilit space that got gradually lower toward the back until the rim rock met the floor of the cavern, exactly like the sloping roof of an attic. There was perpetual twilight back there, cool, shadowy, very grateful after the blazing sun in the front court-yard. When we entered it we heard a soft trickling sound, and we came upon a spring that welled out of the rock into a stone basin and then ran off through a cobble-lined gutter and dripped down the cliffs. I've never anywhere tasted water like it; as cold as ice, and so pure. Long afterward Father Duchene came out to spend a week with us on the mesa; he always carried a small drinking-glass with him, and he used to fill it at the spring and take it out into the sunlight. The water looked like liquid crystal, absolutely colourless, without the slight brownish or greenish tint that water nearly always has. It threw off the sunlight like a diamond.

Beside this spring stood some of the most beautifully shaped water jars we ever found—I gave Mrs. St. Peter one of them—standing there just as if they'd been left yesterday. In the back court we found a great many things besides jars and bowls: a row of grinding-stones, and several clay ovens, very much like those the Mexicans use to-day. There were charred bones and charcoal, and the roof was thick with soot all the way along. It was evidently a kind of common kitchen, where they roasted and baked and probably gossiped. There were corncobs everywhere, and ears of corn with the kernels still on them—little, like popcorn. We found dried beans, too, and strings of pumpkin seeds, and plum seeds, and a cupboard full of little implements made of turkey bones.

Late that afternoon Roddy and I crossed the river and got back to our cabin to rest for a few days.

The second time we went over, we found a long

winding trail leading from the Cliff City up to the top of the mesa—a narrow path worn deep into the stone ledges that overhung the village, then running back into the wood of stunted piñons on the summit. Following this to the north end of the mesa, we found what was left of an old road down to the plain. But making this road passable was a matter of weeks, and we had to get workmen and tools from Tarpin. It was a narrow foot-path, barely wide enough for a sure-footed mule, and it wound down through Black Canyon, dropping in loops along the face of terrifying cliffs. About a hundred feet above the river, it ended— broke right off into the air. A wall of rock had fallen away there, probably from a landslide. That last piece of road cost us three weeks' hard work, and most of our winter's wages. We kept the workmen on long enough to build us a tight log cabin on the mesa top, a little way back from the ledge that hung over the Cliff City.

While we were engaged in road-building, we made a short cut from our cabin down to the Cliff City and Cow Canyon. Just over the Cliff City, there was a crack in the ledge, a sort of manhole, and in this we hung a ladder of pine-trunks spliced together with light chains, leaving the branch forks for foot-holds. By climbing down this ladder we saved about two miles of winding trail, and dropped almost directly into Cow Canyon, where we meant always to leave one of the horses grazing. Taking this route, we could at any time make a quick exit from the mesa—we were used to swimming the river now, and in summer our wet clothes dried very quickly.

Bill Hook, the liveryman at Tarpin, who'd sheltered old Henry when he was down and out, proved a good friend to us. He got our workmen back and forth for us, brought our supplies up on to the mesa on his pack-mules, and when one of us had to stay in town over-night he let us sleep in his hay barn to save a hotel bill. He knew our expenses were heavy, and did everything for us at a bottom price.

By the first of July our money was nearly gone, but we had our road made, and our cabin built on top of the mesa. We brought old Henry up by the new horse-trail and began housekeeping. We were now ready for what we called excavating. We built wide shelves all around our sleeping-room, and there we put the smaller articles we found in the Cliff City. We num-bered each specimen, and in my day-book I wrote down just where and in what condition we had found it, and what we thought it had been used for. I'd got a merchant's ledger in Tarpin, and every night after supper, while Roddy read the newspapers, I sat down at the kitchen table and wrote up an account of the day's work.

Henry, besides doing the housekeeping, was very ea-ger to help us in the "rew-ins," as he called them. He was more patient than we, and would dig with his fingers half a day to get a pot out of a rubbish pile without breaking it. After all, the old man had a wider knowledge of the world than either of us, and it often came in handy. When we were working in a pale pink house, with two stories, and a sort of balcony before the upper windows, we came on a closet in the wall of the upstairs room; in this were a number of curious things, among them a deerskin bag full of little tools. Henry said at once they were surgical instruments; a stone lancet, a bunch of fine bone needles, wooden forceps, and a catheter.

One thing we knew about these people; they hadn't built their town in a hurry. Everything proved their patience and deliberation. The cedar joists had been felled with stone axes and rubbed smooth with sand. The little poles that lay across them and held up the clay floor of the chamber above, were smoothly polished. The door lintels were carefully fitted (the doors were stone slabs held in place by wooden bars fitted into hasps). The clay dressing that covered the stone walls was tinted, and some of the chambers were frescoed in geometrical patterns, one colour laid on another. In one room was a painted border, little tents, like Indian tepees, in brilliant red.

But the really splendid thing about our city, the thing that made it delightful to work there, and must have made it delightful to live there, was the setting. The town hung like a bird's nest in the cliff, looking off into the box canyon below, and beyond into the wide valley we called Cow Canyon, facing an ocean of clear air. A people who had the hardihood to build there, and who lived day after day looking down upon such grandeur, who came and went by those hazardous trails, must have been, as we often told each other, a fine people. But what had become of them? What catastrophe had overwhelmed them?

They hadn't moved away, for they had taken none of their belongings, not even their clothes. Oh, yes, we found clothes; yucca moccasins, and what seemed like cotton cloth, woven in black and white. Never any wool, but sheepskins tanned with the fleece on them. They may have been mountain sheep; the mesa was full of them. We talked of shooting one for meat, but we never did. When a mountain sheep comes out on a ledge hundreds of feet above you, with his trumpet horns, there's something noble about him—he looks like a priest. We didn't want to shoot at them and make them shy. We liked to see them. We shot a wild cow when we wanted fresh meat.

At last we came upon one of the original inhabitants—not a skeleton, but a dried human body, a woman. She was not in the Cliff City; we found her in a little group of houses stuck up in a high arch we called the Eagle's Nest. She was lying on a yucca mat, partly covered with rags, and she had dried into a mummy in that water-drinking air. We thought she had been murdered; there was a great wound in her side, the ribs stuck out through the dried flesh. Her mouth was open as if she were screaming, and her face, through all those years, had kept a look of terrible agony. Part of the nose was gone, but she had plenty of teeth, not one missing, and a great deal of coarse black hair. Her teeth were even and white, and so little worn that we thought she must have been a young woman. Henry named her Mother Eve, and we called her that. We put her in a blanket and let her down with great care, and kept her in a chamber in the Cliff City.

Yes, we found three other bodies, but afterward. One day, working in the Cliff City, we came upon a stone slab at one end of the cavern, that seemed to lead straight into the rock. It was set in cement, and when we loosened it we found it opened into a small, dark chamber. In this there had been a platform, of fine cedar poles laid side by side, but it had crumbled. In the wreckage were three bodies, one man and two women, wrapped in yucca-fibre, all in the same posture and apparently prepared for burial. They were the bodies of old people. We believed they were among the aged who were left behind when the tribe went down to live on their farms in the summer season; that they had died in the absence of the villagers, and were put into this mortuary chamber to await the return of the tribe, when they would have their funeral rites. Probably these people burned their dead. Of course an archæologist could have told a great deal about that civilization from those bodies. But they never got to an archæologist—at least, not on this side of the world.

The first of August came, and everything was going well with us. We hadn't met with any bad luck, and though we had very little money left, there was Blake's untouched savings account in the bank at Pardee, and we had plenty of credit in Tarpin. The merchants there took an interest and were friendly. But the little new moon, that looked so innocent, brought us trouble. We lost old Henry, and in a terrible way. From the first we'd been a little bothered by rattlesnakes—you generally find them about old stone quarries and old masonry. We had got them pretty well cleared out of the Cliff City, hadn't seen one there for weeks. But one Sunday we took Henry and went on an exploring expedition at the north end of the mesa, along Black Canyon. We caught sight of a little bunch of ruins we'd never noticed before, and made a foolhardy scramble to get up to them. We almost made it, and then there was a stretch of rock wall so smooth we couldn't climb it without a ladder. I was the tallest of the three, and Henry was the lightest; he thought he could get up there if he stood on my shoulders. He was standing on my back, his head just above the floor of the cavern, groping for something to hoist himself by, when a snake struck him from the ledge—struck him square in the forehead. It happened in a flash. He came down and brought the snake with him. By the time we picked him up and turned him over, his face had begun to swell. In ten minutes it was purple, and he was so crazy it took the two of us to hold him and keep him from jumping down the chasm. He was struck so near the brain that there was nothing to do. It lasted nearly two hours. Then we carried him home. Roddy dropped down the ladder into Cow Canyon, caught his horse, and rode into Tarpin for the coroner. Father Duchene was preaching there at the mission church that Sunday, and came back with him.

We buried Henry on the mesa. Father Duchene stayed on with us a week to keep us company. We were so cut up that we were almost ready to quit. But he had been planning to come out to see our find for a long while, and he got our minds off our trouble. He worked hard every day. He went over everything we'd done, and examined everything minutely: the pottery, cloth, stone implements, and the remains of food. He measured the heads of the mummies and declared they had good skulls. He cut down one of the old cedars that grew exactly in the middle of the deep trail worn in the stone, and counted the rings under his pocket microscope. You couldn't count them with the unassisted eye, for growing out of a tiny crevice in the rock as that tree did, the increase of each year was so scant that the rings were invisible except with a glass. The tree he cut down registered three hundred and thirty-six years' growth, and it could have begun to grow in that well-worn path only after human feet had ceased to come and go there.

Why had they ceased? That question puzzled him, too. Smallpox, any epidemic, would have left unburied bodies. Father Duchene suggested what Dr. Ripley, in Washington, afterward surmised: that the tribe had been exterminated, not here in their stronghold, but in their summer camp, down among the farms across the river. Father Duchene had been among the Indians nearly twenty years then, he had seventeen Indian pueblos in his parish, and he spoke several Indian dialects. He was able to explain the use of many of the implements we found, especially those used in religious ceremonies. The night before he left us, he summed up the results of his week's study, something like this:

"The two square towers on the mesa top, to which you have given little attention, were unquestionably granaries. Under the stones and earth fallen from the walls, there is a quantity of dried corn on the ear. Not a great harvest, for life must have come to an end here in the summer, when the new crop was not yet garnered and the last year's grain was getting low. The semicircular ridge on the mesa top, which you can see distinctly among the piñons when the sun is low and brings it into high relief, is the buried wall of an amphitheatre, where probably religious exercises and games took place. I advise you not to dig into it. It is probably the most important thing here, and should be left for scholars to excavate.

"The tower you so much admire in the cliff village may have been a watch tower, as you think, but from the curious placing of those narrow slits, like windows, I believe it was used for astronomical observations. I am inclined to think that your tribe were a superior people. Perhaps they were not so when they first came upon this mesa, but in an orderly and secure life they developed considerably the arts of peace. There is evidence on every hand that they lived for something more than food and shelter. They had an appreciation of comfort, and went even further than that. Their life, compared to that of our roving Navajos, must have been quite complex. There is unquestionably a distinct feeling for design in what you call the Cliff City. Buildings are not grouped like that by pure accident, though convenience probably had much to do with it. Convenience often dictates very sound design.

"The workmanship on both the wood and stone of the dwellings is good. The shapes and decoration of the water jars and food bowls is better than in any of the existing pueblos I know, better even than the pottery made at Acoma. I have seen a collection of early pottery from the island of Crete. Many of the geometrical decorations on these jars are not only similar, but, if my memory is trustworthy, identical.

"I see your tribe as a provident, rather thoughtful people, who made their livelihood secure by raising crops and fowl—the great number of turkey bones and feathers are evidence that they had domesticated the wild turkey. With grain in their store-rooms, and mountain sheep and deer for their quarry, they rose gradually from the condition of savagery. With the proper variation of meat and vegetable diet, they developed physically and improved in the primitive arts. They had looms and mills, and experimented with dyes. At the same time, they possibly declined in the arts of war, in brute strength and ferocity.

"I see them here, isolated, cut off from other tribes, working out their destiny, making their mesa more and more worthy to be a home for man, purifying life by religious ceremonies and observances, caring respectfully for their dead, protecting the children, doubtless entertaining some feelings of affection and sentiment for this stronghold where they were at once so safe and so comfortable, where they had practically overcome the worst hardships that primitive man had to fear. They were, perhaps, too far advanced for their time and environment.

"They were probably wiped out, utterly exterminated, by some roving Indian tribe without culture or domestic virtues, some horde that fell upon them in their summer camp and destroyed them for their hides and clothing and weapons, or from mere love of slaughter. I feel sure that these brutal invaders never even learned of the existence of this mesa, honeycombed with habitations. If they had come here, they would have destroyed. They killed and went their way.

"What I cannot understand is why you have not found more human remains. The three bodies you found in the mortuary chamber were prepared for burial by the old people who were left behind. But what of the last survivors? It is possible that when autumn wore on, and no one returned from the farms, the aged banded together, went in search of their people, and perished in the plain.

"Like you, I feel a reverence for this place. Wherever humanity has made that hardest of all starts and lifted itself out of mere brutality, is a sacred spot. Your people were cut off here without the influence of example or emulation, with no incentive but some natural yearning for order and security. They built themselves into this mesa and humanized it."

Father Duchene warmly agreed with Blake that I ought to go to Washington and make some report to the Government, so that the proper specialists would be sent out to study the remains we had found.

"You must go to the Director of the Smithsonian Institution," he said. "He will send us an archæologist who will interpret all that is obscure to us. He will revive this civilization in a scholarly work. It may be that you will have thrown light on some important points in the history of your country."

After he left us, Blake and I began to make definite

plans for my trip to Washington. Blake was to work on the railroad that winter and save as much money as possible. The expense of my journey would be paid out of what we called the jack-pot account, in the bank at Pardee. All our further expenses on the mesa would be paid by the Government. Roddy often hinted that we would get a substantial reward of some kind. When we broke or lost anything at our work, he used to smile and say: "Never mind. I guess our Uncle Sam will make that good to us."

We had a beautiful autumn that year, soft, sunny, like a dream. Even up there in the air we had so little wind that the gold hung on the poplars and quaking aspens late in November. We stayed out on the mesa until after Christmas. We wanted our archæologist, when he came, to find everything in good order. We cleared up any litter we'd made in digging things out, stored all the specimens, even the mummies, in our cabin, and padlocked the doors and windows before we left it. I had written up my day-book carefully to the very end, had even written out some of Father Duchene's deductions. This book I left in concealment on the mesa. I climbed up to the Eagle's Nest in which we had found the mummy of the murdered woman we called Mother Eve, where I had noticed a particularly neat little cupboard in the wall. I put my book in this niche and sealed it up with cement. Mother Eve had greatly interested Father Duchene, by the way. He

laughed and said she was well named. He didn't believe her death could throw any light on the destruc-
tion of her people. "I seem to smell," he said slyly,
"a personal tragedy. Perhaps when the tribe went
down to the summer camp, our lady was sick and
would not go. Perhaps her husband thought it worth
while to return unannounced from the farms some
night, and found her in improper company. The young
man may have escaped. In primitive society the husband is allowed to punish an unfaithful wife with
death."

When the first snow began to fly, we said good-bye
to our mesa and rode into Tarpin. It took several days
to outfit me for my journey to Washington. We bought
a trunk (I'd never owned one in my life), and a supply
of white shirts, an overcoat that was as heavy as lead
and just about as cold, and two suits of clothes. That
conscienceless trader worked off on me a clawhammer
coat he must have had in stock for twenty years. He
easily persuaded Roddy that it was the proper thing for
dress occasions. I think Roddy expected that I would
be received by ambassadors—perhaps I did.

Roddy drew six hundred dollars out of the bank to
stake me, and bought my ticket and Pullman through
to Washington. He went to the station with me the
morning I left, and a hard handshake was good-bye.

For a long while after my train pulled out, I could
see our mesa bulking up blue on the sky-line. I hated

to leave it, but I reflected that it had taken care of itself without me for a good many hundred years. When I saw it again, I told myself, I would have done my duty by it; I would bring back with me men who would understand it, who would appreciate it and dig out all its secrets.

S I X

I got off the train, just behind the Capitol building, one cold bright January morning. I stood for a long while watching the white dome against a flashing blue sky, with a very religious feeling. After I had walked about a little and seen the parks, so green though it was winter, and the Treasury building, and the War and Navy, I decided to put off my business for a little and give myself a week to enjoy the city. That was the most sensible thing I did while I was there. For that week I was wonderfully happy.

My sightseeing over, I got to work. First I went to see the Representative from our district, to ask for letters of introduction. He was cordial enough, but he gave me bad advice. He was very positive that I ought to report to the Indian Commission, and gave me a letter to the Commissioner. The Commissioner was out of town, and I wasted three days waiting about his office, being questioned by clerks and secretaries. They were not very busy, and seemed to find me entertaining. I thought they were interested in my mission, and interest was what I wanted to arouse. I didn't know how influential these people might be—they talked as if they had great authority. I had brought along in my telescope bag some good pieces of pottery—not the best, I was afraid of accident, but some that were representative—and all the photographs Blake and I had taken. We had only a small kodak, and these pictures didn't make much show,—looked, indeed, like grubby little 'dobe ruins such as one can find almost anywhere. They gave no idea of the beauty and vastness of the setting. The clerks at the Indian Commission seemed very curious about everything and made me talk a lot. I was green and didn't know any better. But when one of the fellows there tried to get me to give him my best bowl for his cigarette ashes, I began to suspect the nature of their interest.

At last the Commissioner returned, but he had pressing engagements, and I hung around several days more before he would see me. After questioning me for about half an hour, he told me that his business was with living Indians, not dead ones, and that his office should have informed me of that in the beginning. He advised me to go back to our Congressman and get a letter to the Smithsonian Institution. I packed up my pottery and got out of the place, feeling pretty sore. The head clerk followed me down the corridor and asked me what I'd take for that little bowl he'd taken a fancy to. He said it had no market value, I'd find Washington full of such things; there were cases of them in the cellar at the Smithsonian that they'd never taken the trouble to unpack, hadn't any place to put them.

I went back to my Congressman. This time he wasn't so friendly as before, but he gave me a letter to the Smithsonian. There I went through the same experience. The Director couldn't be seen except by appointment, and his secretary had to be convinced that your business was important before he would give you an appointment with his chief. After the first morning I found it difficult to see even the secretary. He was always engaged. I was told to take a seat and wait, but when he was disengaged he was hurrying off to luncheon. I would sit there all morning with a group of unfortunate people: girls who wanted to get typewriting to do, nice polite old men who wanted to be taken out on surveys and expeditions next summer. The secretary would at last come out with his overcoat on, and would hurry through the waiting-room reading a letter or a report, without looking up.

The office assistants cheered me along, and I kept this up for some days, sitting all morning in that room, studying the patterns of the rugs, and the shoes of the patient waiters who came as regularly as I. One day after the secretary had gone out, his stenographer, a nice little Virginia girl, came and sat down in an empty chair next to mine and began talking to me. She wasn't pretty, but her kind eyes and soft Southern voice took hold of me at once. She wanted to know what I had in my telescope, and why I was there, and where I came from, and all about it. Nearly everyone else had gone out to lunch—that seemed to be the one thing they did regularly in Washington—and we had the waiting-room to ourselves. I talked to her a good deal. Her name was Virginia Ward. She was a tiny little thing, but she had lovely eyes and such gentle ways. She seemed indignant that I had been put off so long after having come so far.

"Now you just let me fix it up for you," she said at last. "Mr. Wagner is bothered by a great many foolish people who waste his time, and he is suspicious. The best way will be for you to invite him to lunch with you. I'll arrange it. I keep a list of his appointments, and I know he is not engaged for luncheon to-morrow. I'll tell him that he is to lunch with a nice boy who has come all the way from New Mexico to inform the Department about an important discovery. I'll tell him to meet you at the Shoreham, at one. That's expensive, but it would do no good to invite him to a cheap place. And, remember, you must ask him to order the luncheon. It will maybe cost you ten dollars, but it will get you somewhere."

I felt grateful to the nice little thing,—she wasn't older than I. I begged her wouldn't she please come to lunch with me herself to-day, and talk to me.

"Oh, no!" she said, blushing red as a poppy. "Why, I'm afraid you think——"

I told her I didn't think anything but how nice she was to me, and how lonesome I was. She went with me, but she wouldn't go to any swell place. She told me a great many useful things.

"If you want to get attention from anybody in Washin'ton," she said, "ask them to lunch. People here will do almost anything for a good lunch."

"But the Director of the Smithsonian, for instance,"

I said, "surely you don't mean that the high-up ones like that——? Why would he want to bother with a cow-puncher from New Mexico, when he can lunch with scientists and ambassadors?"

She had a pretty little fluttery Southern laugh. "You just name a hotel like the Shoreham to the Director, and try it! There has to be somebody to pay for a lunch, and the scientists and ambassadors don't do that when they can avoid it. He'd accept your invitation, and the next time he went to dine with the Secretary of State he'd make a nice little story of it, and paint you up so pretty you'd hardly know yourself."

When I asked her whether I'd better take my pottery—it was there under the table between us—to the Shoreham to show Mr. Wagner, she tittered again. "I wouldn't bother. If you show him enough of the Shoreham pottery, that will be more effective."

The next morning, when the secretary arrived at his office, he stopped by my chair and said he understood he had an engagement with me for one o'clock. That was a good idea, he added: his mind was freer when he was away from office routine.

I had been in Washington twenty-two days when I took the secretary out to lunch. It was an excellent lunch. We had a bottle of Château d'Yquem. I'd never heard of such a wine before, but I remember it because it cost five dollars. I drank only one glass, and that pleased him too, for he drank the rest. Though he was friendly and talked a great deal, my heart sank lower, for he wouldn't let me explain my mission to him at all. He kept telling me that he knew all about the South-west. He had been sent by the Smithsonian to conduct parties of European archæologists through all the show places, Frijoles and Canyon de Chelly, and Taos and the Hopi pueblos. When some Austrian Archduke had gone to hunt in the Pecos range, he had been sent by his chief and the German ambassador to manage the tour, and he had done it with such success that both he and the Director were given decorations from the Austrian Crown, in recognition of his services. Then I had to listen to a long story about how well he was treated by the Archduke when he went to Vienna with his chief the following summer. I had to hear about balls and receptions, and the names and titles of all the people he had met at the Duke's country estate. I was amazed and ashamed that a man of fifty, a man of the world, a scholar with ever so many degrees, should find it worth his while to show off before a boy, and a boy of such humble pretensions, who didn't know how to eat the *hors d'œvres* any more than if an assortment of cocoanuts had been set before him with no hammer.

Imagine my astonishment when, as he was drinking his liqueur, he said carelessly: "By the way, I was successful in arranging an interview with the Director for you. He will see you at four o'clock on Monday."

That was Thursday. I spent the time between then and Monday trying to find out something more about the kind of people I had come among. I persuaded

Virginia Ward to go to the theatre with me, and she told me that it always took a long while to get anything through with the Director, that I mustn't lose heart, and she would always be glad to cheer me up. She lived with her mother, a widow lady, and they had me come to dinner and were very nice to me.

All this time I was living with a young married couple who interested me very much, for they were unlike any people I had ever known. The husband was "in office," as they say there, he had some position in the War Department. How it did use to depress me to see all the hundreds of clerks come pouring out of that big building at sunset! Their lives seemed to me so petty, so slavish. The couple I lived with gave me a prejudice against that kind of life. I couldn't help knowing a good deal about their affairs. They had only a small flat, and rented me one room of it, so I was very much in their confidence and couldn't help overhearing. They asked me not to mention the fact that I paid rent, as they had told their friends I was making them a visit. It was like that in everything; they spent their lives trying to keep up appearances, and to make his salary do more than it could. When they weren't discussing where she should go in the summer, they talked about the promotions in his department; how much the other clerks got and how they spent it, how many new dresses their wives had. And there was always a struggle going on for an invitation to a dinner or a reception, or even a tea-party. When once they got the invitation they had been scheming for, then came the terrible question of what Mrs. Bixby should wear.

The Secretary of War gave a reception; there was to be dancing and a great showing of foreign uniforms. The Bixbys were in painful suspense until they got a card. Then for a week they talked about nothing but what Mrs. Bixby was going to wear. They decided that for such an occasion she must have a new dress. Bixby borrowed twenty-five dollars from me, and took his lunch hour to go shopping with his wife and choose the satin. That seemed to me very strange. In New Mexico the Indian boys sometimes went to a trader's with their wives and bought shawls or calico, and we thought it rather contemptible. On the night of the reception the Bixbys set off gaily in a cab; the dress they considered a great success. But they had bad luck. Somebody spilt claret-cup on Mrs. Bixby's skirt before the evening was half over, and when they got home that night I heard her weeping and reproaching him for having been so upset about it, and looking at nothing but her ruined dress all evening. She said he cried out when it happened. I don't doubt it.

Every cab, every party, was more than they could afford. If he lost an umbrella, it was a real misfortune. He wasn't lazy, he wasn't a fool, and he meant to be honest; but he was intimidated by that miserable sort of departmental life. He didn't know anything else. He thought working in a store or a bank not respectable. Living with the Bixbys gave me a kind of low-spiritedness I had never known before. During my days of waiting for appointments, I used to walk for hours around the fence that shuts in the White House grounds, and watch the Washington monument colour with those beautiful sunsets, until the time when all the clerks streamed out of the Treasury building and the War and Navy. Thousands of them, all more or less like the couple I lived with. They seemed to me like people in slavery, who ought to be free. I remember the city chiefly by those beautiful, hazy, sad sunsets, white columns and green shrubbery, and the monument shaft still pink while the stars were coming out.

I got my interview with the Director of the Smithsonian at last. He gave me his attention, he was interested. He told me to come again in three days and meet Dr. Ripley, who was the authority on prehistoric Indian remains and had excavated a lot of them. Then came an exciting and rather encouraging time for me. Dr. Ripley asked the right sort of questions, and evidently knew his business. He said he'd like to take the first train down to my mesa. But it required money to excavate, and he had none. There was a bill up before Congress for an appropriation. We'd have to wait. I must use my influence with my Representative. He took my pottery to study it. (I never got it back, by the way.) There was a Dr. Fox, connected with the Smithsonian, who was also interested. They told me a good many things I wanted to know, and kept me dangling about the office. Of course they were very kind to take so much trouble with a green boy. But I soon found that the Director and all his staff had one interest which dwarfed every other. There was to be an International Exposition of some sort in Europe the following summer, and they were all pulling strings to get appointed on juries or sent to international congresses—appointments that would pay their expenses abroad, and give them a salary in addition. There was, indeed, a bill before Congress for appropriations for the Smithsonian; but there was also a bill for Exposition appropriations, and that was the one they were really pushing. They kept me hanging on through March and April, but in the end it came to nothing. Dr. Ripley told me he was sorry, but the sum Congress had allowed the Smithsonian wouldn't cover an expedition to the South-west.

Virginia Ward, who had been so kind to me, went out to lunch with me that day, and admitted I had been let down. She was almost as much disappointed as I. She said the only thing Dr. Ripley really cared about was getting a free trip to Europe and acting on a jury, and maybe getting a decoration. "And that's what the Director wants, too," she said. "They don't care much about dead and gone Indians. What they do care about is going to Paris, and getting another ribbon on their coats."

The only other person besides Virginia who was genuinely concerned about my affair was a young Frenchman, a lieutenant attached to the French Embassy, who came to the Smithsonian often on business connected with this same International Exposition. He was nice and polite to Virginia, and she introduced him to me. We used to walk down along the Potomac together. He studied my photographs and asked me such intelligent questions about everything that it was a pleasure to talk to him. He had a fine attitude about it all; he was thoughtful, critical, and respectful. I feel sure he'd have gone back to New Mexico with me if he'd had the money. He was even poorer than I.

I was utterly ashamed to go home to Roddy, dead broke after all the money I'd spent, and without a thing to show for it. I hung on in Washington through May, trying to get a job of some sort, to at least earn my fare home. My letters to Blake had been pretty blue for some time back. If I'd been sensible, I'd have kept my troubles to myself. He was easily discouraged, and I knew that. At last I had to write him for money to go home. It was slow in coming, and I began to telegraph. I left Washington at last, wiser than I came. I had no plans, I wanted nothing but to get back to the mesa and live a free life and breathe free air, and never, never again to see hundreds of little black-coated men pouring out of white buildings. Queer, how much more depressing they are than workmen coming out of a factory.

I was terribly disappointed when I got off the train at Tarpin and Roddy wasn't at the station to meet me. It was late in the afternoon, almost dark, and I went straight to the livery stable to ask Bill Hook for news of Blake. Hook, you remember, had done all our hauling for us, and had been a good friend. He gave me a glad hand and said Blake was out on the mesa.

"I expect maybe he's had his feelings hurt here. He's been shy of this town lately. You see, Tom, folks weren't bothered none about the mesa so long as you fellows were playing Robinson Crusoe out there, digging up curios. But when it leaked out that Blake had got a lot of money for your stuff, then they begun to feel jealous—said them ruins didn't belong to Blake any more than to anybody else. It'll blow over in time; people are always like that when money changes hands. But right now there's a good deal of bad feeling."

I told him I didn't know what he was talking about.

"You mean you ain't heard about the German, Fechtig? Well, Rodney's got some surprise waiting for you! Why, he's had the damnedest luck! He's cleaned up a neat little pile on your stuff."

I begged him to tell me what stuff he meant.

"Why, your curios. This German, Fechtig, come along; he'd been buying up a lot of Indian things out here, and he bought your whole outfit and paid four thousand dollars down for it. The transaction made quite a stir here in Tarpin. I'm not kicking. I made a good thing out of it. My mules were busy three weeks packing the stuff out of there on their backs, and I held the Dutchman up for a fancy price. He had packing cases made at the wagon shop and took 'em up to the mesa full of straw and sawdust, and packed the curios out there. I lost one of my mules, too. You remember Jenny? Well, they were leading her down with a big box on her, and right there where the trail runs so narrow around a bump in the cliff above Black Canyon, she lost her balance and fell clean to the bottom, her load on her. Pretty near a thousand feet, I guess. We never went down to hold a post-mortem, but Fechtig paid for her like a gentleman."

I remember I sat down on the sofa in Hook's office because I couldn't stand up any longer, and the smell of the horse blankets began to make me deathly sick. In a minute I went over, like a girl in a novel. Hook pulled me out on the sidewalk and gave me some whisky out of his pocket flask.

When I felt better I asked him how long this German had been gone, and what he had done with the things.

"Oh, he cleared out three weeks ago. He didn't waste no time. He treated everybody well, though; nobody's sore at him. It's your partner they're turned against. Fechtig took the stuff right along with him, chartered a freight car, and travelled in the car with it. I reckon it's on the water by now. He took it straight through into Old Mexico, and was to load it on a French boat. Seems he was afraid of having trouble getting curiosities out of the United States ports. You know you can take anything out of the City of Mexico."

I had heard all I wanted to hear. I went to the hotel,

got a room, and lay down without undressing to wait for daylight. Hook was to drive me and my trunk out to the mesa early the next morning. All I'd been through in Washington was nothing to what I went through that night. I thought Blake must have lost his mind. I didn't for a minute believe he'd meant to sell me out, but I cursed his stupidity and presumption. I had never told him just how I felt about those things we'd dug out together, it was the kind of thing one doesn't talk about directly. But he must have known; he couldn't have lived with me all summer and fall without knowing. And yet, until that night, I had never known myself that I cared more about them than about anything else in the world.

At the first blink of daylight I jumped up from my damnable bed and went round to the stable to rout Hook out of his bunk. We had breakfast and got out of town with his best team. On the way to the mesa we had a break-down, one of the old dry wheels smashed to splinters. Hook had to unhitch and ride back to Tarpin and get another. Everything took an unreasonably long time, and the afternoon was half gone when he put me and my trunk down at the foot of the Black Canyon trail. Every inch of that trail was dear to me, every delicate curve about the old piñon roots, every chancy track along the face of the cliffs, and the deep windings back into shrubbery and safety. The wild-currant bushes were in bloom, and where the path climbed the side of a narrow ravine, the scent of them in the sun was so heavy that it made me soft, made me want to lie down and sleep. I wanted to see and touch everything, like home-sick children when they come home.

When I pulled out on top of the mesa, the rays of sunlight fell slantingly through the little twisted piñons,—the light was all in between them, as red as a daylight fire, they fairly swam in it. Once again I had that glorious feeling that I've never had anywhere else, the feeling of being *on the mesa,* in a world above the world. And the air, my God, what air!—Soft, tingling, gold, hot with an edge of chill on it, full of the smell of piñons—it was like breathing the sun, breathing the colour of the sky. Down there behind me was the plain, already streaked with shadow, violet and purple and burnt orange until it met the horizon. Before me was the flat mesa top, thinly sprinkled with old cedars that were not much taller than I, though their twisted trunks were almost as thick as my body. I struck off across it, my long black shadow going ahead.

I made straight for the cabin, it was about three miles from the spot where the trail emerged at the top. I saw smoke rising before I could see the hut itself. Blake was in the doorway when I got there. I didn't look at his face, but I could feel that he looked at mine.

"Don't say anything, Tom. Don't rip me up until you hear all about it," he said as I came toward him.

"I've heard enough to about do for me," I blurted out. "What made you do it, Blake? What made you do it?"

"It was a chance in a million, boy. There wasn't any time to consult you. There's only one man in thousands that wants to buy relics and pay real money for them. I could see how your Washington campaign was coming out. I know you'd thought about big figures, so had I. But that was all a pipe dream. Four thousand's not so bad, you don't pick it up every day. And he bore all the expenses. Why, it was a terrible expensive job, getting all that frail stuff out of here. Who else would have bought it, I want to know? We'd have had to pack it around at Harvey Houses, selling it at a dollar a bowl, like the poor Indians do. I took the best chance going, for both of us, Tom."

I didn't say anything, because there was too much to say. I stood outside the cabin until the gold light went blue and a few stars came out, hardly brighter than the bright sky they twinkled in, and the swallows came flying over us, on their way to their nests in the cliffs. It was the time of day when everything goes home. From habit and from weariness I went in through the door. The kitchen table was spread for supper, I could smell a rabbit stew cooking on the stove. Blake lit the lantern and begged me to eat my supper. I didn't go into the bunk-room, for I knew the shelves in there were empty. I heard Blake talking to me as you hear people talking when you are asleep.

"Who else would have bought them?" he kept saying. "Folks make a lot of fuss over such things, but they don't want to pay good money for them."

When I at last told him that such a thing as selling them had never entered my head, I'm sure he thought I was lying. He reminded me about how we used to talk of getting big money from the Government.

I admitted I'd hoped we'd be paid for our work, and maybe get a bonus of some kind, for our discovery. "But I never thought of selling them, because they weren't mine to sell—nor yours! They belonged to this country, to the State, and to all the people. They belonged to boys like you and me, that have no other ancestors to inherit from. You've gone and sold them to a country that's got plenty of relics of its own. You've gone and sold your country's secrets, like Dreyfus."

"That man was innocent. It was a frame-up," Blake murmured. It was a point he would never pass up.

"Whether he's guilty or not, you are! If there was only anybody in Washington I could telegraph to, and have that German held up at the port!"

"That's just it. If there was anybody in Washington that cared a damn, I wouldn't have sold 'em. But you pretty well found out there ain't."

"We could have kept them, then," I told him. "I've got a strong back. I'm not so poor that I have to sell the pots and pans that belonged to my poor grandmothers a thousand years ago. I made all my plans on the train, coming back." (It was a lie, I hadn't.) "I meant to get a job on the railroad and keep our find right here, and come back to it when I had a lay-off. I think a lot more of it now than before I went to Washington. And after a while, when that Exposition is over and the Smithsonian people get home, they would come out here all right. I've learned enough from them so that I could go on with it myself."

Blake reminded me that I had my way to make in the world, and that I wanted to go to school. "That money's in the bank this minute, in your name, and you're going to college on it. You're not going to be a day-labourer like me. After you've got your sheepskin, then you can divide with me."

"You think I'd touch that money?" I looked squarely at him for the first time. "No more than if you'd stolen it. You made the sale. Get what you can out of it. I want to ask you one question: did you ever think I was digging those things up for what I could sell them for?"

Rodney explained that he knew I cared about the things, and was proud of them, but he'd always supposed I meant to "realize" on them, just as he did, and that it would come to money in the end. "Everything does," he added.

"If that nice young Frenchman I met had come down here with me, and offered me four million instead of four thousand, I'd have refused him. There never was any question of money with me, where this mesa and its people were concerned. They were something that had been preserved through the ages by a miracle, and handed on to you and me, two poor cow-punchers, rough and ignorant, but I thought we were men enough to keep a trust. I'd as soon have sold my own grandmother as Mother Eve—I'd have sold any living woman first."

"Save your tears," said Roddy grimly. "She refused to leave us. She went to the bottom of Black Canyon and carried Hook's best mule along with her. They had to make her box extra wide, and she crowded Jenny out an inch or so too far from the canyon wall."

This painful interview went on for hours. I walked up and down the kitchen trying to make Blake understand the kind of value those objects had had for me. Unfortunately, I succeeded. He sat slumping on the bench, his elbows on the table, shading his eyes from the lantern with his hands.

"There's no need to keep this up," he said at last. "You're away out of my depth, but I think I get you. You might have given me some of this Fourth of July talk a little earlier in the game. I didn't know you valued that stuff any different than anything else a fellow might run on to: a gold mine or a pocket of turquoise."

"I suppose you gave him my diary along with the rest?"

"No," said Blake, his voice growing gloomier and darker, "that's in the Eagle's Nest, where you hid it. That's your private property. I supposed I had some share in the relics we dug up—you always spoke of it that way. But I see now I was working for you like a hired man, and while you were away I sold your property."

I said again it wasn't mine or his. He took something out of the pocket of his flannel shirt and laid it on the table. I saw it was a bank passbook, with my name on the yellow cover.

"You may as well keep it," I said. "I'll never touch it. You had no right to deposit it in my name. The townspeople are sore about the money, and they'll hold it against me."

"No they won't. Can't you trust me to fix that?"

"I don't know what I can trust you with, Blake. I don't know where I'm at with you," I said.

He got up and began putting on his coat. "Motives don't count, eh?" he said, his face turned away, as he put his arm into the sleeve.

"They would in anything of our own, between you and me," I told him. "If it was my money you'd lost gambling, or my girl you'd made free with, we could fight it out, and maybe be friends again. But this is different."

"I see. You make it clear." He was quietly stirring around as he spoke. He got his old knapsack off its nail on the wall, opened his trunk and took out some underwear and socks and a couple of shirts. After he had put these into the bag, he slung it over one shoulder, and his canvas water-bag over the other. I let these preparations go on without a word. He went to the

222

cupboard over the stove and put some sticks of choc-
olate into his pocket, then his pipe and a bag of tobacco. Presently I said he'd break his neck if he tried
riding down the trail in the dark.

"I'm not riding the trail," he replied curtly. "I'm
going down the quick way. My horse is grazing in Cow
Canyon."

"I noticed the river's high. It's dangerous crossing,"
I remarked.

"I got over that way a few days ago. I'm surprised
at you, using such common expressions!" he said sar-
castically. *"Dangerous crossing;* it's painted on sign-
boards all over the world!" He walked out of the cabin
without looking back. I followed him to the V-shaped
break in the rim rock, hardly larger than a man's body,
where the spliced tree-trunks made a swinging ladder
down the face of the cliff. I wanted to protest, but only
succeeded in finding fault.

"You'll catch your knapsack on those forks and come
to grief."

"That's my look-out."

By this time my eyes had grown accustomed to the
darkness, and I could see Blake quite clearly—the stub-
born, crouching set of his shoulders that I used to notice when he first came to Pardee and was drinking all
the time. There was an ache in my arms to reach out
and detain him, but there was something else that made
me absolutely powerless to do so. He stepped down
and settled his foot into the first fork. Then he stopped

a moment and straightened his pack, buttoned his coat up to the chin, and pulled his hat on tighter. There was always a night draught in the canyon. He gripped the trunk with his hands. "Well," he said with grim cheerfulness, "here's luck! And I'm glad it's you that's doing this to me, Tom; not me that's doing it to you."

His head disappeared below the rim. I could hear the trees creak under his heavy body, and the chains rattle a little at the splicings. I lay down on the ledge and listened. I could hear him for a long way down, and the sounds were comforting to me, though I didn't realize it. Then the silence closed in. I went to sleep that night hoping I would never waken.

SEVEN

The next morning the whinnying of my saddle-horse in the shed roused me. I took him down to the foot of the trail where I'd left my trunk, and packed my things up to the cabin on his back. I sat up late that night, waiting for Blake, though I knew he wouldn't come. A few days later I rode into Tarpin for news of him. Bill Hook showed me Roddy's horse. He had sold him to the barn for sixty dollars. The station-master told me Blake had bought a ticket to Winslow, Arizona. I wired the station-master and the dispatcher at Winslow, but they could give me no information. Father Duchene came along, on his rounds, and I told him the whole story.

He thought Blake would come back sometime, that I'd only miss him if I went out to look for him. He advised me to stay on the mesa that summer and get ahead with my studies, work up my Spanish grammar and my Latin. He had friends all along the Santa Fé, and he was sure we could catch Blake by advertising in the local papers along the road; Albuquerque, Winslow, Flagstaff, Williams, Los Angeles. After a few days with him, I went back to the mesa to wait.

I'll never forget the night I got back. I crossed the river an hour before sunset and hobbled my horse in the wide bottom of Cow Canyon. The moon was up, though the sun hadn't set, and it had that glittering silveriness the early stars have in high altitudes. The heavenly bodies look so much more remote from the bottom of a deep canyon than they do from the level. The climb of the walls helps out the eye, somehow. I lay down on a solitary rock that was like an island in the bottom of the valley, and looked up. The grey sagebrush and the blue-grey rock around me were already in shadow, but high above me the canyon walls were dyed flame-colour with the sunset, and the Cliff City lay in a gold haze against its dark cavern. In a few minutes it, too, was grey, and only the rim rock at the top held the red light. When that was gone, I could still see the copper glow in the piñons along the edge of the top ledges. The arc of sky over the canyon was silvery blue, with its pale yellow moon, and presently stars shivered into it, like crystals dropped into perfectly clear water.

I remember these things, because, in a sense, that was the first night I was ever really on the mesa at all— the first night that all of me was there. This was the first time I ever saw it as a whole. It all came together in my understanding, as a series of experiments do when you begin to see where they are leading. Something had happened in me that made it possible for me to co-ordinate and simplify, and that process, going on in my mind, brought with it great happiness. It was possession. The excitement of my first discovery was a very pale feeling compared to this one. For me the mesa was no longer an adventure, but a religious emotion. I had read of filial piety in the Latin poets, and I knew that was what I felt for this place. It had formerly been mixed up with other motives; but now that they were gone, I had my happiness unalloyed.

What that night began lasted all summer. I stayed on the mesa until November. It was the first time I'd ever studied methodically, or intelligently. I got the better of the Spanish grammar and read the twelve books of the *Æneid*. I studied in the morning, and in the afternoon I worked at clearing away the mess the German had made in packing—tidying up the ruins to wait another hundred years, maybe, for the right explorer. I can scarcely hope that life will give me another summer like that one. It was my high tide. Every morning, when the sun's rays first hit the mesa top, while the rest of the world was in shadow, I wakened with the feeling that I had found everything, instead of having lost everything. Nothing tired me. Up there alone, a close neighbour to the sun, I seemed to get the solar energy in some direct way. And at night, when I watched it drop down behind the edge of the plain below me, I used to feel that I couldn't have borne another hour of that consuming light, that I was full to the brim, and needed dark and sleep.

All that summer, I never went up to the Eagle's Nest to get my diary—indeed, it's probably there yet. I didn't feel the need of that record. It would have been going backward. I didn't want to go back and unravel things step by step. Perhaps I was afraid that I would lose the whole in the parts. At any rate, I didn't go for my record.

During those months I didn't worry much about poor Roddy. I told myself the advertisements would surely get him—I knew his habit of reading newspapers. There are times when one's vitality is too high to be clouded, too elastic to stay down. Hurrying from my cabin in the morning to the spot in the Cliff City where I studied under a cedar, I used to be frightened at my own heartlessness. But the feel of the narrow moccasin-worn trail in the flat rock made my feet glad, like a good taste in the mouth, and I'd forget all about Blake without knowing it. I found I was reading too fast; so I began to commit long passages of Virgil to memory— if it hadn't been for that, I might have forgotten how to use my voice, or gone to talking to myself. When I look into the *Æneid* now, I can always see two pictures: the one on the page, and another behind that: blue and purple rocks and yellow-green piñons with flat tops, little clustered houses clinging together for protection, a rude tower rising in their midst, rising strong, with calmness and courage—behind it a dark grotto, in its depths a crystal spring.

Happiness is something one can't explain. You must take my word for it. Troubles enough came afterward, but there was that summer, high and blue, a life in itself.

Next winter I went back to Pardee and stayed with the O'Briens again, working on the section and studying with Father Duchene and trying to get some word of Blake. Now that I was back on the railroad, I thought I couldn't fail to find him. I went out to Winslow and to Williams, and I questioned the railroad men. We advertised for him in every possible way, had all the Santa Fé operatives and the police and the Catholic missionaries on the watch for him, offered a thousand dollars reward for whoever found him. But it came to nothing. Father Duchene and our friends down there are still looking. But the older I grow, the more I understand what it was I did that night on the mesa. Anyone who requites faith and friendship as I did, will have to pay for it. I'm not very sanguine about good fortune for myself. I'll be called to account when I least expect it.

In the spring, just a year after I quarrelled with Roddy, I landed here and walked into your garden, and the rest you know.

BOOK THREE

The Professor

O N E

All the most important things in his life, St. Peter
sometimes reflected, had been determined by chance.
His education in France had been an accident. His
married life had been happy largely through a circumstance with which neither he nor his wife had anything
to do. They had been young people with good qualities,
and very much in love, but they could not have been
happy if Lillian had not inherited a small income from
her father—only about sixteen hundred a year, but it
had made all the difference in the world. A few mem-
orable interregnums between servants had let him know
that Lillian couldn't pinch and be shabby and do house-
work, as the wives of some of his colleagues did. Under
such conditions she became another person, and a bitter one.

Tom Outland had been a stroke of chance he
couldn't possibly have imagined; his strange coming,
his strange story, his devotion, his early death and post-
humous fame—it was all fantastic. Fantastic, too, that
this tramp boy should amass a fortune for someone
whose name he had never heard, for "an extravagant
and wheeling stranger." The Professor often thought of
that curiously bitter burst from the barytone in Brahms'
Requiem, attending the words, *"He heapeth up riches
and cannot tell who shall scatter them!"* The vehemence

of this passage had seemed to him uncalled for until he read it by the light of the history of his own family.

St. Peter thought he had fared well with fate. He wouldn't choose to live his life over—he might not have such good luck again. He had had two romances: one of the heart, which had filled his life for many years, and a second of the mind—of the imagination. Just when the morning brightness of the world was wearing off for him, along came Outland and brought him a kind of second youth.

Through Outland's studies, long after they had ceased to be pupil and master, he had been able to experience afresh things that had grown dull with use. The boy's mind had the superabundance of heat which is always present where there is rich germination. To share his thoughts was to see old perspectives transformed by new effects of light.

If the last four volumes of "The Spanish Adventurers" were more simple and inevitable than those that went before, it was largely because of Outland. When St. Peter first began his work, he realized that his great drawback was the lack of early association, the fact that he had not spent his youth in the great dazzling Southwest country which was the scene of his explorers' adventures. By the time he had got as far as the third volume, into his house walked a boy who had grown up there, a boy with imagination, with the training and insight resulting from a very curious experience; who had in his pocket the secrets which old trails and stones and water-courses tell only to adolescence.

Two years after Tom's graduation they took the copy of Fray Garces' manuscript that the Professor had made from the original in Spain, and went down into the South-west together. By autumn they had been over every mile of his trail on horseback. Tom could take a sentence from Garces' diary and find the exact spot at which the missionary crossed the Rio Colorado on a certain Sunday in 1775. Given one pueblo, he could always find the route by which the priest had reached the next.

It was on that trip that they went to Tom's Blue Mesa, climbed the ladder of spliced pine-trees to the Cliff City, and up to the Eagle's Nest. There they took Tom's diary from the stone cupboard where he had sealed it up years ago, before he set out for Washington on his fruitless errand.

The next summer Tom went with the Professor to Old Mexico. They had planned a third summer to-gether, in Paris, but it never came off. Outland was delayed by the formalities of securing his patent, and then came August, 1914. Father Duchene, the mission-ary priest who had been Tom's teacher, stopped in Hamilton on his way back to Belgium, hurrying home to serve in any capacity he might. The rugged old man stayed in Hamilton only four days, but in that time Outland made up his mind, had a will drawn, packed, and said good-bye. He sailed with Father Duchene on the *Rochambeau.*

To this day St. Peter regretted that he had never got that vacation in Paris with Tom Outland. He had wanted to revisit certain spots with him: to go with him some autumn morning to the Luxembourg Gardens, when the yellow horse-chestnuts were bright and bitter after rain; to stand with him before the monument to Delacroix and watch the sun gleam on the bronze figures—Time, bearing away the youth who was struggling to snatch his palm—or was it to lay a palm? Not that it mattered. It might have mattered to Tom, had not chance, in one great catastrophe, swept away all youth and all palms, and almost Time itself.

And suppose Tom had been more prudent, and had not gone away with his old teacher? St. Peter sometimes wondered what would have happened to him, once the trap of worldly success had been sprung on him. He couldn't see Tom building "Outland," or becoming a public-spirited citizen of Hamilton. What change would have come in his blue eye, in his fine long hand with the backspringing thumb, which had never handled things that were not the symbols of ideas? A hand like that, had he lived, must have been put to other uses. His fellow scientists, his wife, the town and State, would have required many duties of it. It would have had to write thousands of useless letters, frame thousands of false excuses. It would have had to "manage" a great deal of money, to be the instrument of a woman who would grow always more exacting. He had escaped all that. He had made something new in the world—and the rewards, the meaningless conventional gestures, he had left to others.

T W O

All those summer days, while the Professor was sending cheerful accounts of his activities to his family in France, he was really doing very little. He had begun, in a desultory way, to annotate the diary that Tom had kept on the mesa, in which he had noted down the details of each day's work among the ruins, along with the weather and anything unusual in the routine of their life. There was a minute description of each tool they found, of every piece of cloth and pottery, frequently accompanied by a very suggestive pencil sketch of the object and a surmise as to its use and the kind of life in which it had played a part. To St. Peter this plain account was almost beautiful, because of the stupidities it avoided and the things it did not say. If words had cost money, Tom couldn't have used them more sparingly. The adjectives were purely descriptive, relating to form and colour, and were used to present the objects under consideration, not the young explorer's emotions. Yet through this austerity one felt the kindling imagination, the ardour and excitement of the boy, like the vibration in a voice when the speaker strives to conceal his emotion by using only conventional phrases.

When the first of August came round, the Professor realized that he had pleasantly trifled away nearly two months at a task which should have taken little more than a week. But he had been doing a good deal besides—something he had never before been able to do.

St. Peter had always laughed at people who talked about "day-dreams," just as he laughed at people who naïvely confessed that they had "an imagination." All his life his mind had behaved in a positive fashion. When he was not at work, or being actively amused, he went to sleep. He had no twilight stage. But now he enjoyed this half-awake loafing with his brain as if it were a new sense, arriving late, like wisdom teeth. He found he could lie on his sand-spit by the lake for hours and watch the seven motionless pines drink up the sun. In the evening, after dinner, he could sit idle and watch the stars, with the same immobility. He was cultivating a novel mental dissipation—and enjoying a new friendship. Tom Outland had not come back again through the garden door (as he had so often done in dreams!), but another boy had: the boy the Professor had long ago left behind him in Kansas, in the Solomon Valley—the original, unmodified Godfrey St. Peter.

This boy and he had meant, back in those far-away days, to live some sort of life together and to share good and bad fortune. They had not shared together, for the reason that they were unevenly matched. The young St. Peter who went to France to try his luck, had a more active mind than the twin he left behind in the Solomon Valley. After his adoption into the Thierault household, he remembered that other boy very rarely, in moments of home-sickness. After he met Lillian Ornsley, St. Peter forgot that boy had ever lived.

But now that the vivid consciousness of an earlier state had come back to him, the Professor felt that life with this Kansas boy, little as there had been of it, was the realest of his lives, and that all the years between had been accidental and ordered from the outside. His career, his wife, his family, were not his life at all, but a chain of events which had happened to him. All these things had nothing to do with the person he was in the beginning.

The man he was now, the personality his friends knew, had begun to grow strong during adolescence, during the years when he was always consciously or unconsciously conjugating the verb "to love"—in society and solitude, with people, with books, with the sky and open country, in the lonesomeness of crowded city streets. When he met Lillian, it reached its maturity. From that time to this, existence had been a catching at handholds. One thing led to another and one development brought on another, and the design of his life had been the work of this secondary social man, the lover. It had been shaped by all the penalties and responsibilities of being and having been a lover. Because there was Lillian, there must be marriage and a salary. Because there was marriage, there were children. Because there were children, and fervour in the blood and brain, books were born as well as daughters. His histories, he was convinced, had no more to do with his original ego than his daughters had; they were a result of the high pressure of young manhood.

The Kansas boy who had come back to St. Peter this summer was not a scholar. He was a primitive. He was only interested in earth and woods and water. Wherever sun sunned and rain rained and snow snowed, wherever life sprouted and decayed, places were alike to him. He was not nearly so cultivated as Tom's old cliff-dwellers must have been—and yet he was terribly wise. He seemed to be at the root of the matter; Desire under all desires, Truth under all truths. He seemed to know, among other things, that he was solitary and must always be so; he had never married, never been a father. He was earth, and would return to earth. When white clouds blew over the lake like bellying sails, when the seven pine-trees turned red in the declining sun, he felt satisfaction and said to himself merely: "That is right." Coming upon a curly root that thrust itself across his path, he said: "That is it." When the maple-leaves along the street began to turn yellow and waxy, and were soft to the touch,—like the skin on old faces,— he said: "That is true; it is time." All these recognitions gave him a kind of sad pleasure.

When he was not dumbly, deeply recognizing, he was bringing up out of himself long-forgotten, unimportant memories of his early childhood, of his mother, his father, his grandfather. His grandfather, old Napoleon Godfrey, used to go about lost in profound, continuous meditation, sometimes chuckling to himself. Occasionally, at the family dinner-table, the old man would try to rouse himself, from motives of politeness, and would ask some kindly question—nearly always absurd and often the same one he had asked yesterday. The boys used to shout with laughter and wonder what profound matters could require such deep meditation, and make a man speak so foolishly about what was going on under his very eyes. St. Peter thought he was beginning to understand what the old man had been thinking about, though he himself was but fifty-two, and Napoleon had been well on in his eighties. There are only a few years, at the last, in which man can consider his estate, and he thought he might be quite as near the end of his road as his grandfather had been in those days.

The Professor knew, of course, that adolescence grafted a new creature into the original one, and that the complexion of a man's life was largely determined by how well or ill his original self and his nature as modified by sex rubbed on together.

What he had not known was that, at a given time, that first nature could return to a man, unchanged by all the pursuits and passions and experiences of his life; untouched even by the tastes and intellectual activities which have been strong enough to give him distinction among his fellows and to have made for him, as they say, a name in the world. Perhaps this reversion did not often occur, but he knew it had happened to him, and he suspected it had happened to his grandfather. He did not regret his life, but he was indifferent to it. It seemed to him like the life of another person.

Along with other states of mind which attended his realization of the boy Godfrey, came a conviction (he did not see it coming, it was there before he was aware of its approach) that he was nearing the end of his life. This conviction took its place so quietly, seemed so matter-of-fact, that he gave it little thought. But one day, when he realized that all the while he was preparing for the fall term he didn't in the least believe he would be alive during the fall term, he thought he might better see a doctor.

The family doctor knew all about St. Peter. It was summer, moreover, and he had plenty of time. He devoted several mornings to the Professor and made tests of the most searching kind. In the end he of course told St. Peter there was nothing the matter with him.

"What made you come to me, any discomfort or pain?"

"None. I simply feel tired all the time."

Dr. Dudley shrugged. "So do I! Sleep well?"

"Almost too much."

"Eat well?"

"In every sense of the word, well. I am my own *chef.*"

"Always a *gourmet,* and never anything wrong with your digestive tract! I wish you'd ask me to dine with you some night. Any of that sherry left?"

"A little. I use it plentifully."

"I'll bet you do! But why did you think there was something wrong with you? Low in your mind?"

"No, merely low in energy. Enjoy doing nothing. I came to you from a sense of duty."

"How about travel?"

"I shrink from the thought of it. As I tell you, I enjoy doing nothing."

"Then do it! There's nothing the matter with you. Follow your inclination."

St. Peter went home well satisfied. He did not mention to Dr. Dudley the real reason for his asking for a medical examination. One doesn't mention such things. The feeling that he was near the conclusion of his life was an instinctive conviction, such as we have when we waken in the dark and know at once that it is near morning; or when we are walking across the country and suddenly know that we are near the sea.

Letters came every week from France. Lillian and Louie alternated, so that one or the other got off a letter to him on every fast boat. Louie told him that wherever they went, when they had an especially delightful day, they bought him a present. At Trouville, for instance, they had laid in dozens of the brilliant rubber casquettes he liked to wear when he went swimming. At Aix-les-Bains they found a gorgeous dressing-gown for him in a Chinese shop. St. Peter was happy in his mind about them all. He was glad they were there, and that he was here. Their generous letters, written when there were so many pleasant things to do, certainly deserved more than one reading. He used to carry them out to the lake to read them over again. After coming out of the water he would lie on the sand, holding them in his hand, but somehow never taking his eyes off the pine-trees, appliquéd against the blue water, and their ripe yellow cones, dripping with gum and clustering on the pointed tips like a mass of golden bees in swarming-time. Usually he carried his letters home unread.

His family wrote constantly about their plans for next summer, when they were going to take him over with them. Next summer? The Professor wondered. . . . Sometimes he thought he would like to drive up in front of Notre Dame, in Paris, again, and see it standing there like the Rock of Ages, with the frail generations breaking about its base. He hadn't seen it since the war.

But if he went anywhere next summer, he thought it would be down into Outland's country, to watch the sunrise break on sculptured peaks and impassable mountain passes—to look off at those long, rugged, untamed vistas dear to the American heart. Dear to all hearts, probably—at least, calling to all. Else why had his grandfather's grandfather, who had tramped so many miles across Europe into Russia with the Grande Armée, come out to the Canadian wilderness to forget the chagrin of his Emperor's defeat?

F O U R

The fall term of the university opened, and now the Professor went to his lectures instead of to the lake. He supposed he did his work, he heard no complaints from his assistants, and the students seemed interested. He found, however, that he wasn't willing to take the trouble to learn the names of several hundred new students. It wasn't worth while. He felt that his relations with them would be of short duration.

The McGregors got home from their vacation in Oregon, and Scott was much amused to find the Professor so doggedly anchored in the old house.

"It never struck me, Doctor, that you were a man who would be keeping up two establishments. They'll be coming home pretty soon, and then you'll have to decide where you are going to live."

"I can't leave my study, Scott. That's flat."

"Don't, then! Darn it, you've a right to two houses if you want 'em."

This encounter took place on the street in front of the house. The Professor went wearily upstairs and lay down on the couch, his refuge from this ever-increasing fatigue. He really didn't see what he was going to do about the matter of domicile. He couldn't make himself believe that he was ever going to live in the new house again. He didn't belong there. He remembered some lines of a translation from the Norse he used to read long ago in one of his mother's few books, a little two-volume Ticknor and Fields edition of Longfellow, in blue and gold, that used to lie on the parlour table:

> For thee a house was built
> Ere thou wast born;
> For thee a mould was made
> Ere thou of woman camest.

Lying on his old couch, he could almost believe himself in that house already. The sagging springs were like the sham upholstery that is put in coffins. Just the equivocal American way of dealing with serious facts, he reflected. Why pretend that it is possible to soften that last hard bed?

He could remember a time when the loneliness of death had terrified him, when the idea of it was insupportable. He used to feel that if his wife could but lie in the same coffin with him, his body would not be so insensible that the nearness of hers would not give it comfort. But now he thought of eternal solitude with gratefulness; as a release from every obligation, from every form of effort. It was the Truth.

One morning, just as St. Peter was leaving the house to go to his class-room, the postman handed him two letters, one addressed in Lillian's hand and one in Louie's. He put them into his pocket. The feel of them disturbed him. They were of a suspicious thinness—as if they didn't contain amusing gossip, but announced sudden decisions. He set off down the street, sniffing the lake-cooled morning air and trying to overcome a feeling of nervous dread.

All the morning those two letters lay in his breast pocket. Though they were so light, their effect was to make him drop his shoulders and look woefully tired. The weather, too, had changed, come on suddenly hot and sultry at noon, as if getting ready for a storm. When his classes were over and he was back in his study again, St. Peter felt no interest in lunch. He took out the two letters and ripped them open with his forefinger to have it over. Yes, all plans were changed, and by the happiest of expectations. The family were hurrying home to prepare for the advent of a young Marsellus. They would sail on the sixteenth, on the *Berengaria*.

Lillian added a postscript to the effect that by this same mail she was getting off a letter to Augusta, who would come to him for the keys of the new house. She would be the best person to open the house and arrange to have the cleaning done. She would take it entirely off his shoulders and see that everything was properly put in order.

They were sailing on the sixteenth, and this was the seventeenth; they were already on the water. The *Berengaria* was a five-day boat. St. Peter caught up his hat and light overcoat and started down the stairs. Halfway down, he stopped short, went back to his study, and softly shut the door behind him. He sat down, forgetting to take off his overcoat, though the afternoon was so hot and his face was damp with perspiration. He sat motionless, breathing unevenly, one dark hand lying clenched on his writing-table. There must, he was repeating to himself, there must be some way in which a man who had always tried to live up to his responsibilities could, when the hour of desperation came, avoid meeting his own family.

He loved his family, he would make any sacrifice for them, but just now he couldn't live with them. He must be alone. That was more necessary to him than anything had ever been, more necessary, even, than his marriage had been in his vehement youth. He could not live with his family again—not even with Lillian. Especially not with Lillian! Her nature was intense and positive; it was like a chiselled surface, a die, a stamp upon which he could not be beaten out any longer. If her character were reduced to an heraldic device, it would be a hand (a beautiful hand) holding flaming arrows—the shafts of her violent loves and hates, her clear-cut ambitions.

"In great misfortunes," he told himself, "people want to be alone. They have a right to be. And the misfortunes that occur within one are the greatest. Surely the saddest thing in the world is falling out of love—if once one has ever fallen in."

Falling out, for him, seemed to mean falling out of all domestic and social relations, out of his place in the human family, indeed.

St. Peter did not go out of the house that afternoon.

He did not leave his study. He sat at his desk with bent head, reviewing his life, trying to see where he had made his mistake, to account for the fact that he now wanted to run away from everything he had intensely cared for.

Late in the afternoon the heaviness of the air in the room drove him to the window. He saw that a storm was coming on. Great orange and purple clouds were blowing up from the lake, and the pine-trees over about the Physics laboratory were blacker than cypresses and looked contracted, as if they were awaiting something. The rain broke, and it turned cold.

The rain-storm was over in half an hour, but a heavy blow had set in for the night. The wind would be a protection, he thought. Even Augusta would hardly come plodding up the stairs to-night. It seemed strange to be dreading Augusta, but just now he did dread her. He believed he was safe, for to-night. Though it was only five o'clock, the sky was black, and the room was dusky and chilly. He lit the stove and lay down on the couch. The fire made a flickering pattern of light on the wall. He lay watching it, vacantly; without meaning to, he fell asleep. For a long while he slept deeply and peacefully. Then the wind, increasing in violence, disturbed him. He began to be aware of noises—things banging and slamming about. He turned over on his back and slept deeper still.

When St. Peter at last awoke, the room was pitch-black and full of gas. He was cold and numb, felt sick and rather dazed. The long-anticipated coincidence had happened, he realized. The storm had blown the stove out and the window shut. The thing to do was to get up and open the window. But suppose he did not get up——? How far was a man required to exert himself against accident? How would such a case be decided under English law? He hadn't lifted his hand against himself—was he required to lift it for himself?

At midnight St. Peter was lying in his study, on his box-couch, covered up with blankets, a hot water bottle at his feet; he knew it was midnight, for the clock of Augusta's church across the park was ringing the hour. Augusta herself was there in the room, sitting in her old sewing-chair by the kerosene lamp, wrapped up in a shawl. She was reading a little much-worn religious book that she always carried in her handbag. Presently he spoke to her.

"Just when did you come in, Augusta?"

She got up and came over to him.

"Are you feeling comfortable, Doctor St. Peter?"

"Oh, very, thank you. When did you happen in?"

"Not any too soon, sir," she said gravely, with a touch of reproof. "You never would take my cautions about that old stove, and it very nearly asphyxiated you. I was barely in time to pull you out."

"You pulled me out, literally? Where to?"

"Into the hall. I came over in the storm to ask you for the keys of the new house—I didn't get Mrs. St. Peter's letter until I got home from work this evening, and I came right over. When I opened the front door I smelled gas, and I knew that stove had been up to its old tricks. I supposed you'd gone out and forgot to turn it off. When I got to the second floor I heard a fall overhead, and it flashed across me that you were up here and had been overcome. I ran up and opened the two windows at the head of the stairs and dragged you out into the wind. You were lying on the floor." She lowered her voice. "It was perfectly frightful in here."

"I seem to remember Dudley's being here."

"Yes, after I'd turned off the stove and opened everything up, I went next door and telephoned for Doctor Dudley. I thought I'd better not say what the trouble was, but I asked him to come at once, as you'd been taken ill. You soon came round, but you were flighty." Augusta hurried over her recital. She was evidently embarrassed by the behaviour of the stove and the condition in which she had found him. It was an ugly accident, and she didn't want the neighbours to know of it.

"You must have great presence of mind, Augusta, and a strong arm as well. You say you found me on the floor? I thought I was lying here on the couch. I remember waking up and smelling gas."

"You were stupefied, but you must have got up and tried to get to the door before you were overcome. I was on the second floor when I heard you fall. I'd never heard anyone fall before, that I can remember, but I seemed to know just what it was."

"I'm sorry to have given you a fright. I hope the gas hasn't made your head ache."

"All's well that ends well, as they say. But I doubt

if you ought to be talking, sir. Could you go to sleep again? I can stay till morning, if you prefer."

"I'd be greatly obliged if you would stay the night with me, Augusta. It would be a comfort. I seem to feel rather lonely—for the first time in months."

"That's because your family are coming home. Very well, sir."

"You do a good deal of this sort of thing—watching and sitting up with people, don't you?"

"Well, when I happen to be sewing in a house where there's sickness, I am sometimes called upon."

Augusta sat down by the table and again took up her little religious book. St. Peter, with half-closed eyes, lay watching her—regarding in her humankind, as if after a definite absence from the world of men and women. If he had thought of Augusta sooner, he would have got up from the couch sooner. Her image would have at once suggested the proper action.

Augusta, he reflected, had always been a corrective, a remedial influence. When she sewed for them, she breakfasted at the house—that was part of the arrangement. She came early, often directly from church, and had her breakfast with the Professor, before the rest of the family were up. Very often she gave him some wise observation or discreet comment to begin the day with. She wasn't at all afraid to say things that were heavily, drearily true, and though he used to wince under them, he hurried off with the feeling that they were good for him, that he didn't have to hear such sayings half often enough. Augusta was like the taste of bitter herbs; she was the bloomless side of life that he had always run away from,—yet when he had to face it, he found that it wasn't altogether repugnant. Sometimes she used to telephone Mrs. St. Peter that she would be a day late, because there had been a death in the family where she was sewing just then, and she was "needed." When she met him at the table the next morning, she would look just a little more grave than usual. While she ate a generous breakfast, she would reply to his polite questions about the illness or funeral with befitting solemnity, and then go readily to another topic, not holding the dolorous note. He used to say that he didn't mind hearing Augusta announce these deaths which seemed to happen so frequently along her way, because her manner of speaking about it made death seem less uncomfortable. She hadn't any of the sentimentality that comes from a fear of dying. She talked about death as she spoke of a hard winter or a rainy March, or any of the sadnesses of nature.

It occurred to St. Peter, as he lay warm and relaxed but undesirous of sleep, that he would rather have Augusta with him just now than anyone he could think of. Seasoned and sound and on the solid earth she surely was, and, for all her matter-of-factness and hardhandedness, kind and loyal. He even felt a sense of obligation toward her, instinctive, escaping definition, but real. And when you admitted that a thing was real, that was enough—now.

He didn't, on being quite honest with himself, feel any obligations toward his family. Lillian had had the best years of his life, nearly thirty, and joyful years they had been, nothing could ever change that. But they were gone. His daughters had outgrown any great need of him. In certain wayward moods Kitty would always come to him. But Rosamond, on that shopping expedition in Chicago, had shown him how painful the paternal relation could be. There was still Augusta, however; a world full of Augustas, with whom one was outward bound.

All the afternoon he had sat there at the table where now Augusta was reading, thinking over his life, trying to see where he had made his mistake. Perhaps the mistake was merely in an attitude of mind. He had never learned to live without delight. And he would have to learn to, just as, in a Prohibition country, he supposed he would have to learn to live without sherry. Theoretically he knew that life is possible, may be even pleasant, without joy, without passionate griefs. But it had never occurred to him that he might have to live like that.

Though he had been low-spirited all summer, he told the truth when he told Dr. Dudley that he had not been melancholy. He had no more thought of suicide than he had thought of embezzling. He had always regarded it as a grave social misdemeanour—except when it occurred in very evil times, as a form of protest. Yet when he was confronted by accidental extinction, he had felt no will to resist, but had let chance take its way, as it had done with him so often. He did not remember springing up from the couch, though he did remember a crisis, a moment of acute, agonized strangulation.

His temporary release from consciousness seemed to have been beneficial. He had let something go—and it was gone: something very precious, that he could not consciously have relinquished, probably. He doubted whether his family would ever realize that he was not the same man they had said good-bye to; they would be too happily preoccupied with their own affairs. If his apathy hurt them, they could not possibly be so much hurt as he had been already. At least, he felt the ground under his feet. He thought he knew where he was, and that he could face with fortitude the *Berengaria* and the future.

ABOUT THE AUTHOR

Willa Cather was born near Winchester, Virginia, in 1873. When she was ten years old, her family moved to the prairies of Nebraska, later the setting for a number of her novels. At the age of twenty-one she graduated from the University of Nebraska and spent the next few years doing newspaper work and teaching high school in Pittsburgh. In 1903 her first book, *April Twilights,* a collection of poems, was published, and two years later *The Troll Garden,* a collection of stories, appeared in print. After the publication of her first novel, *Alexander's Bridge,* in 1912, Cather devoted herself full time to writing, and, over the years, completed eleven more novels (including *O Pioneers!, My Ántonia, The Professor's House,* and *Death Comes for the Archbishop*), four collections of short stories, and two volumes of essays. Cather won the Pulitzer Prize for *One of Ours* in 1923. She died in 1947.

___ The Romance of Tristan and Iseult by Joseph Bedier	$9.00	0-679-75016-9
___ A Lost Lady by Willa Cather	$9.00	0-679-72887-2
___ Collected Stories by Willa Cather	$14.00	0-679-73648-4
___ Death Comes for the Archbishop by Willa Cather	$9.00	0-679-72889-9
___ My Ántonia by Willa Cather	$8.00	0-679-74187-9
___ My Mortal Enemy by Willa Cather	$8.95	0-679-73179-2
___ O Pioneers! by Willa Cather	$9.00	0-679-74362-6
___ One of Ours by Willa Cather	$12.00	0-679-73744-8
___ The Professor's House by Willa Cather	$10.00	0-679-73180-6
___ Forty Stories by Anton Chekhov, translated by Robert Payne	$12.00	0-679-73375-2
___ A Tale of Two Cities by Charles Dickens, with an introduction by Simon Schama	$7.95	0-679-72965-8
___ The Brothers Karamazov by Fyodor Dostoevsky, translated by Richard Pevear and Larissa Volokhonsky	$16.00	0-679-72925-9
___ Crime and Punishment by Fyodor Dostoevsky, translated by Richard Pevear and Larissa Volokhonsky	$14.00	0-679-73450-3
___ The Aeneid, translated by Robert Fitzgerald	$8.00	0-679-72952-6
___ The Odyssey, translated by Robert Fitzgerald	$8.00	0-679-72813-9
___ Madame Bovary by Gustave Flaubert, translated by Francis Steegmuller	$11.00	0-679-73636-0
___ Three Classic African-American Novels, edited and with an introduction by Henry Louis Gates, Jr. Clotel by William Wells Brown, Iola Leroy by Frances E.W. Harper, The Marrow of Tradition by Charles W. Chesnutt	$15.00	0-679-72742-6
___ The Sorrows of Young Werther by Johann Wolfgang von Goethe, translated by Elizabeth Mayer and Louise Bogan, with a foreword by W. H. Auden	$10.00	0-679-72951-8

___ **The Ink Dark Moon: Love Poems** $10.00   0-679-72958-5
by Ono No Komachi and Izumi Shikibu,
Women of the Ancient Court of Japan,
     translated by Jane Hirshfield with Mariko Aratani

___ **The Panther and the Lash** by Langston Hughes $10.00   0-679-73659-X

___ **Selected Poems of Langston Hughes** $10.00   0-679-72818-X
by Langston Hughes

___ **The Ways of White Folks** by Langston Hughes $9.00   0-679-72817-1

___ **Stories** by Katherine Mansfield, $12.00   0-679-73374-4
     with an introduction by Jeffrey Meyers

___ **The Republic of Plato**, translated by B. Jowett $9.00   0-679-73387-6

___ **Cyrano de Bergerac** by Edmond Rostand, $9.95   0-679-73413-9
     translated by Anthony Burgess

___ **The Tale of Genji** by Murasaki Shikibu, $11.00   0-679-72953-4
     translated and abridged by Edward Seidensticker

___ **Dr. Jekyll and Mr. Hyde** by Robert Louis Stevenson, $7.00   0-679-73476-7
     with an introduction by Joyce Carol Oates

___ **Democracy in America: Volume I** $12.00   0-679-72825-2
by Alexis de Tocqueville,
translated by Phillips Bradley,
with an introduction by Daniel J. Boorstin

___ **Democracy in America: Volume II** $12.00   0-679-72826-0
by Alexis de Tocqueville,
translated by Phillips Bradley

___ **Narrative of Sojourner Truth** $9.00   0-679-74035-X
by Sojourner Truth,
edited and with an introduction by
Margaret Washington

___ **Germinal** by Émile Zola $8.00   0-679-75430-X